LOOK TO THE RIVER

NUMBER EIGHT IN THE TEXAS TRADITION SERIES

James W. Lee, General Editor

Look to the River

William A. Owens

Afterword by Tom Pilkington

Texas Christian University Press
Fort Worth

Library of Congress Cataloging-in-Publication Data
Owens, William A., 1905-
Look to the river.
(Texas tradition series ; no. 8)
I. Title. II. Series.
PS365.W58L66 1988 813'.52 87-40267
ISBN 0-87565-076-7
0-87565-026-0 (pbk.)

Illustrations by Walle Conoly

For Ann

INTRODUCTION

The stimulus for *Look to the River* came out of a personal experience when I was about fifteen. A chain gang road crew had a tent in a pasture nearby. At night another boy and I would go to hear the convicts sing and watch them dance. Black men and white men shackled in ball and chain sat or lay on a double row of cots. The white cap'n sat with his gun across his lap and a bloodhound at his feet. One by one a trusty would take a man's ball and chain off and make him sing or dance for the cap'n. Emotional energy began building in me at the time. It took me nearly fifty years to write it out of me.

In several attempts I wrote myself in as a white boy, Jed, on the chain gang. In early drafts the impact was on him alone. Later I added Luster, a black boy the same age, also chained to a cot and not likely to get free because he was black. Any draft I wrote was static. Something was missing. Suddenly I knew I needed Old John, a Jewish peddler who came along our road summer and fall. With the possible synthesis, the story moved rapidly. I wrote the first draft in three weeks on my lunch hour, the second in six, also on my lunch hour. Old John made a climax to the story and added the essential compassion. I made it as southern as I could with dialect and by taking out all words of Latin derivation I could find.

William A. Owens

From *The Texas Literary Tradition*

LOOK TO THE RIVER

1

"Corn and blackbirds don't mix," Basil had said the first morning the young corn began to show through the red sandy earth. "They don't mix a-tall, unless'n it's in the blackbird's craw."

He said it half-jokingly, as he said most things. Then he set Jed, his bound boy, to drive the blackbirds from the cornfield.

"I'll have me a stand of corn," he said, his voice grim, his blue eyes lighter with the laughter behind them, "or I'll have me a strip of your hide."

So every morning as soon as it was daylight, before the sun came up to warm the air, Jed took a long cane pole with a white flour sack tied on it like a flag and went to the cornfield to keep the blackbirds from pulling up the green shoots sprouting from yellow grains. With the taste of side meat and flour gravy still in his mouth, he went out to the long rows of corn—rows nearly a mile long, stretching over sandy knoll after sandy knoll and ending in a brushy turnrow. In the gray light he could see the blackbirds settling between him and the gray bushes. With the pole in the air and the flour sack flapping, he ran the length of the rows crying, "Shoo, blackbirds, shoo, blackbirds." Sometimes, in his anger, his voice rose on *shoo* and broke into a shrill sound, and the birds circled away black and light as leaves.

It was March, the time of southwest winds and northwest winds. If the wind was southwest, it was warm and soft, drifting in from the Gulf of Mexico over miles and miles of fresh-plowed fields, fresh with the smell of flowers. If it was northwest, it brought fine dust, left from the sandstorms on the Great Plains—dust that changed the sky from bright blue to reddish brown and the sun to a red ball that Jed could watch with his naked eye. Whichever way the wind blew, it brought blackbirds, millions of them, on their way north, swooping and swirling in masses of pepper-black specks, or coming to earth and covering the young green of oaks and grass with their glossy blackness.

Basil, in the next field, with two mules to the plow bedding for cotton, kept an eye on Jed and the blackbirds. A cloud of them could settle all at once on the cornfield. In five minutes they could ruin the stand and he would have to plant over. In five minutes they could throw his work and crops out of season, and he would be too far behind to catch up in a year.

"It's a light job you've got," he said, "keeping them out, but I reckon you'll be worth your hire all right if you save the corn."

Basil didn't often talk about the bounding, but it was there between them for Jed to remember and think about from one end of the row to the other.

In January he had come walking up the road from the Red River bottoms, asking for work and board at every farmhouse he passed, telling people he was old enough to work out, and big enough, if they would hire him, big enough to handle a team and cultivator like a man.

It was middle of an afternoon when, after a night in the woods and hours of walking, he came to Basil's place.

"Hello," he called from the gate, afraid he would find no one at home and no telling how far to the next house. The doors and windows were shut tight, and the open hallway between the two front rooms was bare.

"Hello," he called again, and was turning to go when the front door of the fireplace room opened and Basil put his head out.

"Light and hitch."

He's joking me, Jed thought. He sees me afoot and makes out like I'm on horseback.

"I cain't light," Jed said. "I'm on shanks' mare."

Better to answer a joke with a joke.

"Well, come in anyway. We don't bite."

Jed lifted the gate latch and went across a strip of bare yard.

Basil waited in the open door, big and reddish of hair and skin.

"Basil's my handle. What's yourn?"

"Jed."

He could have said *Jedediah Johnson* but he had a feeling the name belonged to what he had left behind. There was little enough to leave behind and less to bring out: only himself and the clothes on his back.

"Well, come in by the fire, Jed, so I can shut the door."

Basil led him into a room dark except for light from one small window and the glow of a fire burned down to ashy-white coals. A woman sat by the window carding cotton. On one side she had a bag of lint; on the other a stack of white fluffy batts on a chair.

"The old woman, Jed."

She leaned toward him and pushed her sunbonnet back from her face, letting the light fall on her dark eyes and pale cheeks.

"Howdy, Jed."

Her voice was loud and twangy.

"Howdy, ma'am."

She went on carding, tearing at a mat of lint on her carding combs. When the teeth of one comb were covered white she held it tight on one knee and, working with the other, with quick pulls and light pushes, fluffed the lint into a batt. She laid the batt on the stack and pressed it down lightly.

"Nigh on time for quilting," she said.

Basil brought a chair for Jed and punched the fire to a pile of flaming chunks. For a time there was only the ripping cloth sound of carding and the solid tick of the mantel clock.

"You come far?" the woman asked.

"Down the road a ways." No need to tell her how far unless she asked. "Down in the bottoms. We kind of run out'n work and I come up this way looking for me a job." He looked at Basil. "You wouldn't be needing a hand, would you?"

In the silence brought by his question he looked at them and wished he could stay with them awhile, till he caught up with himself enough to move on. They were kind people, he could tell by their faces. He wanted to tell them at once that he was really on his way outside, that the stay at any place would not be long, that any job he took would have to be left when the itch to go got strong. He wanted to tell them the truth, but he was afraid they would look cross and say they had no place for him. He wanted them to know without telling them that he was too tired and hungry to go another step on the road.

Basil poked the fire again and measured him from head to toe, like measuring a work horse.

"I could use a boy," he said, with a tone of bargaining in his voice. "I ain't got nothing to work but me and the old woman. She's stout as e'er a man, but she cain't do the housework and go to the field, too. Say I was to hire you. Would you stay with me till crops is gathered? Say till October?"

Basil knew enough about Jed already to know he would have to move on. Without being told, he knew. It saved Jed from having to tell him.

"How much'll you pay me?"

"Fifty cents a day and board is customary around here, not counting Saturday e'ening and Sunday."

Jed figured it in his head. Fifty cents a day from January to October. Not counting days lost Saturday e'enings and Sundays, he would save enough money to travel a long ways—maybe as far as Dallas, and that was as far as he meant to go. He wanted the job, and he would keep from telling them where he would go in October. He would take the job, but first he had his own bargaining to do.

"I've got only what I'm wearing," he said to Basil, "so I'll need me a few clothes to take the job. How much you aiming to give me for bounding me?"

Basil looked at the woman, who had pushed her sunbonnet back on her shoulders.

"What do you think, Cannie?"

She looked at Jed sharply.

"You running off from home, Jed?"

"No, ma'am. I ain't got nothing left to run off from. If I was I would tell you."

"I'll take your word, Jed, till I know different." She turned to Basil. "Maybe a month for bounding?"

"A month's pay then, Jed. Twelve dollars, not counting Saturday e'enings and Sundays. That'll get you some duckings and shoes from the catalogue."

Jed had a hard time keeping to his chair. He never expected anybody to give that much bounding money.

"It's a heap better here'n in the bottoms," he said. "I hired out lots o' times down there, but couldn't make enough to get a grounding. Folks cropping on the shares cain't pay their hands much."

He looked at the woman and then at Basil, to make sure they meant it.

"I'll take it, and be beholden to you."

Basil laughed.

"You may not feel so beholden when you've stood in with me long enough to see the work we've got to do. About then you may want to jump traces—"

"Not till October. I'm bound to stay hitched till October."

The bargain made, the woman spoke again.

"Jed can sleep in the shed room." She laid her carding combs on the stack of batts and brushed the lint from her skirt. "I'll get it ready. It's got a good cot in it. Ain't nobody slept in it since old peddler John was here last. When he comes agin, I'll spread you a pallet on the floor."

For the first time she smiled at Jed.

"I ain't got nothing agin you calling me Cannie."

So Jed had come to work for Basil and Cannie. The first night Basil gave him twelve dollars and Cannie got out the catalogue and helped him fill out his order for clothes. All this was done at the kitchen table, after the supper dishes had been cleared away. Basil thought Jed should wait and buy from the peddler but Cannie, looking at his clothes, offered to meet the mail carrier for him and buy the money order.

Then Jed took a lamp and, shielding the flame against the

wind with his hand, went out on the porch and through the hall to the shed room. He found a cot, a stool, and an old trunk for storing clothes, when the new ones came. Too late to go back for it, he remembered that he had left the catalogue on the kitchen table. Basil had called it the wish book. Jed wanted to wish himself asleep over pictures of the things he could buy with what was left of his bounding money.

Jed liked working with Basil in the woods or in the barn, talking with him, listening to the jokes that made them men together. He liked playing checkers and dominoes with him before the fire at night. He did not mind helping Cannie on rainy days putting a new quilt in the frames. He liked hearing them talk about him when they sat around the fire together.

"Jed's might nigh like one of us, ain't he, Basil?" Cannie said before he had been with them a week.

"Might nigh. Almost like we borned him."

Of the outside jobs, there was nothing he did not like, mostly because of Basil. Basil was as big as a skinned mule, and twice as stout. He knew how to heft a job so that he took the heavy end and left the light end to Jed. He knew how to knock off work before Jed got too worn out trying to keep up with him.

Inside, there was only one thing—the sound of Cannie singing alto. Every summer she sang alto in singing school. All winter long she practiced her notes, singing not the tune but the alto part. Jed never liked music much anyway, and when it came like the steady drone of a broken-winged bumblebee he hated it. When the weather was too bad for outside jobs, he and Basil stayed out of sound of her voice, shelling corn in the crib or picking peanuts off the dried vines in the hayloft.

January passed quickly, and then February. The bounding money went for new things from the catalogue. So did the pay for February. Jed kept to himself his plans for moving on. Days at a time passed when they did not enter his mind. Nights, alone in the shed room, he looked at the place as his own.

Then came March and the blackbirds. In a week of minding

them, Jed hated them more than anything he had ever known. He had never heard of anything as plaguey as blackbirds. When he was at one end of the field, catching his breath, they flocked to the other, and he had to run as hard as he could, waving his flour sack and yelling at the top of his voice. When he was almost upon them they rose up chattering and circled toward another part of the field. Sometimes they waited in the oak trees till he had to walk away to test them. Then they swooped down, and he had to go running again. The scarecrow he built of Cannie's dress and bonnet flapped in the wind but did not bother them at all. They lit on the broomstick arms, and from there settled down on the corn. Basil just laughed when he told him how pesky they were; so there was nothing for him to do but run back and forth from daylight till dark shouting his angry cries.

A farm hand has a right to rest at dinnertime, but he had no rest. Every morning he watched Cannie hang a dish towel on the lilac bush by the kitchen, the signal for Basil to come to dinner. He wanted to go to the house and eat with them, as he had before, but the oaks were full of blackbirds. He had to wait for Basil to bring his dinner to the field. It was a pesky job, belonging rightly to girls and women, but Basil would not let him off from it. As he ran up and down the rows he knew again that he had to leave in October. He vowed he would never be bound to a farm again. His mind made up, he ran and shouted and thought of the time when he would be as free as the blackbirds.

2

Toward the end of the second week of blackbirds the wind was from the southwest, soft and warm and sweet. Jed felt the laziness of spring. The blackbirds seemed to feel it too. They chattered and preened themselves in the oak trees with no eye at all for the young corn running in thin green lines to the ends of the rows. Jed sat on a knoll in the middle of the field with the pole stuck in the ground beside him and the flour sack waving in the breeze. He passed the time by taking off his shoes and piling mounds of soft warm earth over his winter-white feet and pressing it down with his hands. When he took his feet away he left little caves that he could thrust his hands into. He looked at the oaks again. The blackbirds had gone, without a sound to let him know that they were leaving. Barefoot, he walked to the end of the field, toughening his feet as he had every spring as long as he could remember.

When the sun was a hand high he watched Basil unhitch his mules and drive them toward the barn. Sunset would come fast, and then dusk. At first dark he could go to the house.

A long line of blackbirds came from the south, in a wavy flow with regular dips and rises. They were headed north, and the line soon stretched from horizon to horizon. Basil had told him they roosted at night in the canebrakes along the Red River. Jed tried to guess how many blackbirds would be waiting for them in the canebrakes. He wondered how far north their next stop would be. They went on and on, not knowing, he thought, how lucky they were not to be bounden.

When he looked toward the house again he saw a two-horse buggy turning in. It was a sturdy rig, and the man on the seat held the horses steady over the rough ruts. He was a round lump under a wide gray hat. Behind him was another lump, a big bale wrapped in black and tied with ropes. Jed raced to the end of the field nearest the house to get a closer look. It must be old peddler John, he thought, on his way north with the spring, like Basil said. He watched Basil go out and shake hands with the man and help him unhitch his team. He watched the men and horses go out of sight under the barn shed. Then, when dusk still had not deepened to dark, he raced the length of the field again, shouting at the blackbirds any nonsense that came into his head.

When he came down the field again it was first dark, and there was no sound of blackbirds in the oak trees. He had run till there were pinpricks of pain in his legs, but he kept on running, feeling the lightness of his feet, the thumping of his shoes slung over his shoulder.

At the back porch he stopped long enough to wet his face and hands and dry them on a roller towel. He put on his shoes without lacing them and went quietly through the hall. The front door was open and a hickory fire flamed on the hearth. Basil sat on one side of the chimney place, the peddler on the other. The oilcloth-wrapped bale lay behind him on the floor.

"John," Basil said, "you ain't seen Jed yet. He's working for me this year. It ain't like he was a hired hand, but he stays with me and helps me out."

"Glad to know you." The peddler held out his hand. He said *glad* like *glot*. A Dutchman, Basil had said before. Whatever he was, Jed knew, he was from outside home territory. But he was friendly in his blue eyes and weathered face, though he looked like a dude with his gray hair and gray suit, his maroon socks and tie to match, and a white handkerchief in his breast pocket.

"Yep," Basil said, "Jed come up out'n the swamps holler to the toes. I filled him up on grub, and he's making me a good hand for a boy. Right now I got him minding the blackbirds out'n the corn till it gets big enough they cain't hurt it."

John looked Jed over carefully.

"He looks like a good boy, yes. He going back to the bottoms when you get through with him?"

Basil shook his head.

"He ain't said, but I reckon not. I reckon he ain't got much to go back to. I ain't never laid eyes on the place he come from, but I know he's better off here than there with no folks nor nobody to go back to."

Jed knew from the peddler's eyes that he was being sized up, as Basil had sized him up, and he knew he could tell the peddler things he had never told Basil and Cannie. He waited for John to speak to him, to give him a chance to tell why he was never going back to the bottoms, but the chance did not come.

"You know," Basil said, "I've always laid off to ask you how you got the name John. It's a kind of funny name for you to have, with your Dutchman's brogue and all—"

"It's always that. I never changed the first part. Only in Bavaria where I was born it was pronounced *Johann*. When I got to France they called me *Jean*. In Spain it was *Juan*. Here it's *John*, but it's still the same name."

Basil laughed.

"You been kicked outa all them places?"

John looked sad a moment, but was beginning to laugh with Basil when Jed burst out.

"You *been* in all them places?"

John turned to him and the laughter left his eyes.

"Them, and plenty more."

He said it with a kind of sadness in his voice.

"Tell me about them," Jed said. "What's it like where you've been?"

"Wait a minute, Jed," Basil said. "When you come in, John was telling me about the crops. He's come up all the way from the Gulf of Mexico with the spring. It ain't likely I'll get to talk to somebody else that's seen so much of this year's farming. How is crops where you've been, John?"

Crops. Farming.

Jed had never seen a man so stuck on crops and farming. Basil would pass up anything to talk about crops and farming. Old John would as lief talk about all the places he had been, if only Basil would give him a chance.

Glad though for any word from outside, Jed settled on a stool in the rim of the firelight and listened while John talked of what he had seen farmers doing, naming people and places Jed had never heard of. While he was talking, Cannie was in the kitchen cooking supper and singing over and over the alto part of "Bury Me Beneath the Willow," making it sound like—as Basil sometimes said—the tune the cow died on. Her steps from table to stove were quick. She wanted to get through supper so the peddler could show his goods.

"You going on down the road tomorrow?" Basil asked when John had reported all he could on crops and farming. "You won't see much farming till you get way down in the bottoms, nigh about where Jed come from."

"No, I'm turning back toward town. People down that way won't even have egg money this time o' year."

"Then where you going?" Jed asked.

"North again. I'll hit the ferry across Red River and keep going north."

"I seen blackbirds going north this e'ening," Jed said. "You going where they're going?"

John laughed.

"Depends on the weather and how I feel."

Jed had to let Basil and Cannie know that when the time came he was moving on.

"I'd feel like keeping on going. I'd cross the river and not take time to rest in the canebrakes."

Cannie was coming toward the door to the fireplace room, finishing up the words she had been through a dozen times already: "And when he knows where I lay sleeping perhaps he will then think of me."

The tune ended on a reedy note.

"Supper's ready," she said. "Come and get it or I'll throw it out."

At the table, after the laughter over her joke, Cannie looked at Jed.

"I heard what you said about going, Jed. You ain't aiming to leave us, after we been so good to you?"

"I—"

She did not wait for him to finish.

"You cain't. You're bounden to stay." She turned to the peddler. "I always say to Basil it was a good thing we took him in, bounden. The Lord only knows the trouble he might a got in if'n it hadn't been for us. I hope you're listening to me, Jed."

He wanted to tell her that all of her talk of trouble would not keep him from going when the time came, but the look in her face told him to keep quiet.

"I'm listening."

He said it in a way that pleased her. She leaned toward him and smiled.

"Better make haste with supper. I cain't wait to look inside the peddler's pack."

After supper, while Basil and John had cups of coffee in the fireplace room, Cannie trimmed the wicks of the coal-oil lamps and set them on the table and mantel. Jed saw she had put the catalogue away and was glad. No need for John to feel bad because they wished on the catalogue.

When they had gathered by the fire, John rolled his bale to the middle of the floor and carefully untied the ropes. Then he folded the oilcloth back from neatly tied boxes and bundles. The room was suddenly filled with the smells of new cotton cloth, and of soaps, spices, and perfumes. Jed moved in closer—close enough to touch, if he dared, anything in the pack.

Cannie and Basil had been through this before. They sat in their chairs, stooped, waiting. John opened a box of hard candies and passed it to them. Jed watched so hard that John raised his eyes and smiled at him.

"Want a candy, son?"

"Yes, sir."

With the candy between his tongue and cheek, Jed watched the peddler untie a stack of dress goods, each piece cut to length for a dress, each a different pattern and with colors truer than anything he had seen in the catalogue. As he held each one up Cannie cried, "Ain't that a purty one? I'd sure like to have me a dress out'n that."

She went back through the stack to a green-flowered print and fingered it again. John unfolded it and spread it over his pack.

"That'd make a nice dress for you, ma'am."

"I wish I could—"

She stopped and looked quickly at Basil. He said *no* with a shake of his head.

"I'm not asking you to buy it, ma'am," John said. "I'm giving it to you. You had extra work cooking for me—"

Basil stopped him.

"You know we ain't charging you nothing, John. It wouldn't be right, us charging you—"

"I know you don't, but I always like to give something to the woman. She works hard."

When Basil said she could have it, Cannie measured the piece and held it against her thigh. Then she folded it and sat smoothing it with her fingers.

"It's a heap nicer goods than the one you give me last time," she said.

John went through his pack, opening all the boxes, giving them the pleasure of seeing things they would never think of buying. Cannie brought out her egg money and bought powder for herself and pink soap for Sunday. Basil laughed and said that John would have to come back in the fall, after cotton had been sold, to get any money out of him.

In one of the boxes there was a nickel-plated pocket watch with a big black dial. John wound it, looked at the clock on the mantel, and set it. Jed could hear it ticking, light and fast—not like the slow, heavy sound of the clock. John handed the watch to Basil.

"Good vatch," he said. "You better buy."

Basil held the watch to his ear.

"How much?"

"For you, I make it three dollars—"

"Three dollars? What do you think I'm made of? Money?"

He turned the watch over in his hand and gave it back to John. "You'll have to come agin on that one."

From the moment he saw it, Jed wanted the watch more than he had ever wanted anything. If he had it, he would never have to wait for Cannie to put the towel out to tell the time of day. He could take it out of his pocket any time and listen to the friendly ticking. When he was almost to the point of reaching for it, John put it back in the box. Jed watched it go, afraid to ask to see it when he did not have three dollars to pay for it.

John came at last to the bottom of the pack, and they had seen more goods than they could buy with a year's cropping. Then, one by one, he put the bundles together again and tied them with string. All the time, Jed's mind was on the watch—on owning the watch. He made up his mind to buy it in the fall, when his time was up and he was paid off. But not now. Basil would laugh at him if he asked for money to buy it now.

When the pack was all tied again John slung it on his back and, with Basil leading the way with a lamp, took it to the shed room. Jed followed them through the hall.

"Jed, your pallet's made on the floor," Cannie called to him. "Go to bed quiet and get up quiet so's not to keep John awake."

Jed passed the door to the shed room and waited in the back yard for John to get undressed and into bed. Then he came in and blew out the lamp. In the darkness he took off his clothes down to his underwear and crawled under the quilt on the pallet.

Basil had stopped him from asking John about faraway places. Basil was not with them now to stop him from asking John questions, or from talking about the things he had never told Basil and Cannie. There was no one to keep him from talking, and he was afraid. He had nothing to go on but his feeling that John would understand his longing to see and know. He was quiet a long time before he was able to try what he believed.

"John."

He said it in a voice that did not sound like his own.

"Yes, Jed."

He waited for John to say more, but there was only the sound of his slow, heavy breathing.

"What's it like in Spain?" he asked when he thought John was going to sleep.

"It's beautiful."

He did not sound sleepy now.

"And in France?"

"It's beautiful, too."

"What about Germany?"

"It's the most beautiful of all."

Jed thought of the sun shining bright on rows of green young corn.

"More beautiful than here?"

"Much more. It was the place of my childhood. You are not yet old enough to know what it means to a man, the place of his childhood. Every year it becomes more beautiful."

"Why did you leave?" He asked the question and, without taking time to think, followed it with another. "Is it like Basil said? Did you—did you have to leave because of trouble?"

He could hear John sigh under his breath.

"It was that, and it wasn't. You wouldn't understand maybe. I did not belong. I could never belong. Someone, sometime, must have made me know I would never belong. It is a trick of the memory to make us forget the badness of the people and remember the goodness of the land. It is now all beautiful."

Suddenly he laughed.

"It was also something in me. I always had to move on. Then I got here and it is free like I always wanted. I got with the peddling a good living, and I never have to stay any place long enough to be in anybody's way. I got always the spring and the fall. In the spring I go north with the sun. In the fall I go south, down to the Gulf of Mexico, where it's always flowers and sunshine. Like the gypsies, I got it in the blood to go."

It was like Jed's thoughts, put in words better than he could say them.

"John?"

"Yes, Jed."

"I got something to tell you. It's like Basil said. I come up out'n the bottoms. He don't know why. He ain't ast and I ain't told him. He knows I didn't have nobody left to belong to. He don't know I've got something in me that makes me have to move on. Him and Cannie talks like I'm never going another step up the road. You want to know what I know?"

"Yes, Jed."

Jed sat up on his pallet and talked. All the things he had not told Basil and Cannie came out, as fast as he could say them: the life he had left in the Red River bottoms, Cannie's nagging alto, the blackbirds that made his days hateful to him, and over and over the need to move on. He stopped, feeling that he had said more than he should have said to anyone.

He heard the cot creak and knew John was sitting up.

"When I was a boy in Germany I was like you," John said. "I wanted always to go—to see—so I left everything behind and went. I saw it all—France, Spain, and then America. I never stopped, and I never will. I don't need to stop, and I'm afraid to. I'll keep on going as long as somebody needs a peddler—"

Jed could not wait for him to finish.

"John, could I go with you? Could I be your hired hand, John?"

He felt nothing but the blackness around him and the sound of his sharp breathing as he waited for John to answer.

"Tomorrow?" John asked. "Tomorrow morning early?"

Jed remembered his bounding.

"No, not tomorrow. I'm bound to Basil and cain't go tomorrow. I sure wisht I could. I'd liefer work for you than any man I ever seen."

"When will you be free?"

"October, when the crops are in. I'll be free to go then."

"October, *hein?* I'll be coming by here on my way south again.

You'll be free to go then?"

"Yes, sir."

"Basil won't mind?"

"He'll mind, I reckon, not getting any work out'n me, but I won't be bounden to him any longer. How can he keep me if I ain't bounden to him?"

"I don't blame Basil for not wanting to lose a good boy. If you can settle it with him so you won't leave with hard feelings, you be ready when I come back. The things we'll see—me and you in the buggy. I'll take you down to Dallas. I'll take you all the way to the Gulf of Mexico. When winter comes we'll be down by the Rio Grande—me and you by ourselves, riding along in the buggy, stopping to sell what people want to buy, never staying any place longer'n we want to."

Jed threw off the quilt and stood up on his pallet. He heard John swing around and set his bare feet on the bare floor.

"I'd be thankful to go with you, sir."

"You don't need to feel thankful, son. I been needing a boy to help me. The bale's getting too heavy for my shoulders. It's a bargain, Jed, between you and me. Your side is to be ready to go. My side is to take you with me."

Jed needed something to bind the bargain. He trusted John, but he needed something as a reminder when John was not there.

"John?" he asked in a whisper.

"Yes, Jed."

"John, don't you want to give me something to hold me bounden to you?"

"Give you something? You mean money?"

"No, sir, I ain't asking for money. I just want something from you that will make me feel bounden. You know what it's like to feel bounden?"

John laughed.

"I'm the dumbhead. I should have thought of it, but it's been so long since I was with a boy I forgot. We do need to feel bounden, Jed. You know something I could give you?"

Jed felt the water in his mouth.

"Yes, sir. When you had the pack open you showed Basil a watch. I'd be bounden to you for that watch."

"You mean it? It's a cheap watch. You can have it."

"Tonight?"

"It's in the pack."

"Cain't we open the pack?"

John waited a moment before speaking.

"If we had a light."

Jed slid his feet over the floor till he found his overalls. He took a match from his pocket and lit the lamp. John, in long cotton underwear, got up from the cot and knelt beside the pack. Jed knelt beside him and held the lamp close while he untied the ropes and folded back the oilcloth. John lifted out the stack of boxes.

"There," Jed whispered. "It's that one."

He put a finger on a box far down in the stack.

"How'd you know?"

"I watched you put it there."

With a good-humored smile, John slipped the box out and opened it. He took the watch out and held it close for Jed to hear the ticking.

"It's a good watch," Jed said. "I ain't never had me a watch before."

John took a gold watch from the stand by his cot and checked one against the other for time. Then he held one to each ear to listen to the ticking. He handed one to Jed.

"Here. It ticks good."

Jed held the watch in his hand and studied the dial.

"I'm beholden to you, John. Now I can wait till October. You can count on me being here when you come in October."

John tied up the bale and stretched out on the cot.

"You'd better put out the light and go to sleep, Jed. The blackbirds'll be after the corn at daylight."

Jed put out the light and crawled under the quilt again. But he was not ready to think of sleep. In the darkness the hands and numbers on the dial glowed with the brilliance of stars in the north sky. Tomorrow he would shoo off the blackbirds and not mind it.

He would do his job without thinking about it. He would have too many other things in his mind.

The ticking, under the quilt, was like the steady hammering of his heart, marking off the time till October. With the watch in his hand he could wait out the time till his bounding would be over. Then he would go, like the blackbirds—only he would be going south with old John. He laughed at the blackbirds. They were no longer hateful to him.

3

Before daylight, Jed heard Basil tapping on the door and calling softly.

"Get rolling, Jed. It's soon day, and the blackbirds'll be at the corn. Don't wake John. He ain't got no call to be out so early."

Jed put on his shirt and overalls and sat on his pallet to lace his shoes. When he was ready to go, he took the watch from his pillow and studied the glowing hands and numbers.

"Nigh on to five o'clock," he whispered to himself. "It'll be day in no time a-tall. I got to get hustling."

He tried the watch in the watch pocket and felt the bulge it made on his overalls. Basil and Cannie would see it there. They would see it and ask questions he did not want to answer. He opened the trunk and hid it on the bottom, under his clothes.

He looked at John on the cot by the window, hidden under a roll of quilts, sleeping quietly. He wanted to wake him and talk to him about what it would be like in October—when they would go off together in October. But Basil had said not to wake him, and he was still bounden to Basil. He closed the door behind him and went shivering through the hall.

Cannie was in the kitchen putting wood in the stove. Jed ran his hands through the steam of the teakettle to take the chill off.

"Biscuits is done, Jed," Cannie said. "You and Basil go on and eat. I've got to fix a snack for old John to take on the road. He ain't ast for it, but I'd hate to see him go off without'n something for his dinner."

Jed sat at the table with Basil and thought of John on the road in his buggy, rolling along, eating the biscuits and ham and green-grape pie Cannie was packing in a shoe box. She tied the box with a string and then brought her dress goods from the fireplace room. She held it in the lamplight and passed her fingers through the loose folds.

"I don't mind doing for old John," she said. "Ten years he's been a-coming here, regular as the calendar, and he ain't never failed once to give me something. They ain't many folks with goods to sell that gives any of it away. They mostly hang on to it like they don't know the hankerings of other people."

Basil slid his hand down a fold of cloth.

"I reckon he's about the best old Dutchman I ever seen, and I'd tell him that to his face." He leaned back and slapped his knee. "But I wouldn't tell him I ain't never seen another Dutchman."

Jed slipped his fingers into his watch pocket. The watch was not there, but he could feel where it had rounded out the pocket. He was thinking that he knew things about John that Basil and Cannie would never know—things he would always keep to himself. He looked at Basil and Cannie. They expected him to say something.

"I ain't never seen nobody like him down in the bottoms," he said.

Basil laughed.

"You won't see many like him anywhere. They ain't no place he ain't been, and he knows everything there is to know about peddling. It took him a heap o'years to learn all he knows—a heap o' years and a heap o' wandering. I hate to think how many buggies he's wore out going up and down the road, in sun and rain. I reckon it's what he wants."

"I reckon so," Cannie said in her flat voice. "He's sure welcome to it. It sure must take grit to keep going."

The lamplight grew pale in a flush from the eastern sky.

"Better get to the field," Basil said. "Blackbirds'll be swarming with the first light."

"Cain't I stay long enough to help old John hitch up?"

Basil was firm.

"Nothing doing. It could cost me a good crop o' corn."

Knowing he meant it, Jed went at a trot under oak trees filled with birds restless with the dawn. He took the pole with the flour sack and ran the length of the field shooing away birds circling to light.

When the sun was nearly a hand high he saw John hitching his horses to the buggy. He ran down the field as close as he could to the house and watched him bring out the bale of goods and lash it on behind the seat. He wanted to go to him, to tell him again he would be waiting in October, but Cannie came out to the buggy with the shoe box under her arm. He knew what she would say if she saw him leave the cornfield.

John put the shoe box on the seat beside him and drove away slowly over the rough rutted road. It was the road to town. Thirty miles on that road north to the ferry, and on and on north. When Jed no longer expected it, John looked across the cornfield and waved to him with the buggy whip. When he saw the flour sack flapping, he dropped the whip in the socket and went out of sight around a bend in the road.

The sun, bright and warm, climbed up a deep blue sky. Jed sat in the middle of the field with the flour sack waving above him and watched another line of blackbirds passing in flight. He could almost see the corn growing. He tried to content himself with the thought that the days would pass one on top of the other—that he would get the work done he had bound for, and then he would go.

"I was meant to go," he told himself. "If I wasn't, I'd a had something to hold me back. Outside o' what I owe Basil and Cannie, I ain't got nothing nor nobody to stop me from going."

Most people are kept tied down by something, he thought, but not me.

"It's like I been give a sign."

The sign was that, one by one, he had been freed of everything. Last of all the house he had lived in. When the house that had been home was home no longer, he had started on the road. It was a shack, not big enough or good enough to be called a house, but with his father and mother in it he could think of it as home. Not now, or ever. It would always be the shack as he had seen it: half hid in the morning fog when he went to the fields at daybreak

—or the unpainted walls baked yellow gray in the summer sun—or dark gray in winter against the whitish gray of cottonwoods.

Before it lay the wide red fields of the Red River bottoms—cotton fields where men, white and black, worked with mules and plows to get the ground broke and the cotton planted, fields where the women and children came to work at chopping time and picking time. Jed felt the aching arms from hoeing, the shoulders tired from pulling a cotton sack over the red earth. Behind it lay a wide band of tall cottonwoods which shut off the bluff and river, and the scraggly brush of the Oklahoma side.

It was the river that first set his mind on going. Hoeing or picking, he could look to the river and think of what it was like to be in a skiff on the river. He could go up the river, down the river, or across to Oklahoma. He saw only woods and brakes in Oklahoma, but they were different from the woods and fields around his house. He had a different feeling just to be in Oklahoma. He heard talk of the ones that had left by the river.

"They'll come back," the hands in the fields said. "Them that's drunk a drop o' Red River water always comes back.

Not me, he thought. Once I'm gone, I'm never coming back. Wild horses couldn't drag me.

Then the changes came, one upon the other, and he was free to go wherever he wanted to go.

His father had been the first, dead of swamp fever, after weeks of chills that shook his body, of fevers that wet his body and made him talk strange words. One morning he was dead, and Negroes sent by the overseer from the big barns brought lumber and built a box for him. When it was late in the day, with the box in the wagon, with his mother beside him on the straight board seat, Jed had driven the narrow road through fields of corn and cotton his father had plowed, to the graveyard in the sand hills. White men from the fields and commissary lowered the box and piled a mound of sand over it. When they had gone, he and his mother marked "J. J." on a board and set it in the mound of earth. Then he stopped at the commissary to say he was old enough and strong enough to carry on his father's work.

The work was hard, but he kept up, through summer and winter. While it was still winter he was on the board seat again, with another coffin in the wagon behind him. His mother had not seemed sick when he went to work in the morning. When he came in for dinner she had dropped her tired body on the bed and died without a word to him. The men were there to lower the coffin and mound the earth. The women who had laid her in the coffin stood with bowed heads and wet eyes.

The burying over, Jed went to the commissary for the evening up. The man who kept the books was not one to waste time on words. By spring Jed would have to give up the house he called home. He could make the account square by giving up the things in it. After that, he would be like the other hands, working to get enough ahead to be on his own.

One morning toward the end of winter plowing he went to the barns before daylight to harness the team he was working. He looked at the mules, red roan in the lantern light, and knew he would never take them out of the stall again. Nothing bound him to stay. There was no one but the overseer to say he could not go.

He hid out all day, taking a last look at the house, at the river, making up his mind not to leave by the river. He drank from the river, dipping the red water up in his hat brim, filling himself so he would never have to come back for another taste. At the graveyard he marked "M. J." on the board and under the initials "1910." Then he set the board between the two graves.

That night he started walking, without telling anyone he was going, and he was afraid to look back. Someone might see him and try to hold him. He felt the road under his feet change from red gum to sand. After a time he heard the wind in the pine trees and knew he had left the bottoms behind him. When the moon was high and he could see how the road wound through the pine trees, he stopped by a creek and built a fire on the sand. He had never seen pines before. It was worth coming so far to be able to lie on his back and watch the fire light up the underside of limbs high abovc him.

4

Je-ed. Oh, Jed."

He heard Basil calling from the house and saw him and Cannie standing close together in the back yard. The dish towel was on the lilac bush. He looked at the sun. It was not time for dinner, but Cannie had put the dish towel on the lilac bush to call them in. Wondering what they wanted with him, he took up the cane pole and ran down the field.

They were still standing in the yard when he ran up, out of breath. Something was wrong. He could see it in their faces—Basil's darker red under the sunburn, Cannie's dead white under her sunbonnet—and in the accusing look in their eyes.

Just when he was going to ask what had happened, Basil came toward him, holding out the watch.

"That's old John's watch," he said. For the first time Jed saw him angry, and with no joking in his voice. "How'd you get it? Did you steal it?"

Before Jed could answer, Cannie spoke.

"I was moving the clothes in your trunk and found it—hid like it was stole. I called Basil in and ast him. He didn't know nothing about it. I said to him, 'Jed must a taken it. He wouldn't a hid it if he hadn't a taken it.' "

She pushed back her sunbonnet and glared at him with eyes that said he'd better tell the truth.

"John give it to me," Jed said in a low voice. "He took it out'n the box and give it to me."

Basil came close enough for him to hear the ticking.

"How come he give it to you? You ain't nothing to him. He never seen you before yistiddy. You'd better tell me the truth."

Jed knew they would have the truth out of him—the things he had wanted to keep from them till October.

"He just give it to me—"

"What for?"

"To bound me—"

"To bound you? He cain't. You're bounden to me—"

Cannie did not wait for him to stop.

"Don't that beat all you ever heard tell of. First us, then him. Ain't no telling how many other people he's put on before he got here."

Jed had to tell them.

"It ain't for now. He's bounden me to go with him in the fall, when I ain't beholden to you no longer. I ain't breaking my word to you now."

He saw a look pass between Basil and Cannie.

"You'd better say that," Basil said. "I laid out money on you. I'll have it back, or I'll have it out'n your hide. Cannie heard our bargain."

Cannie ran a wet tongue over her pale lips.

"We'uns been good to you, Jed. We didn't know you from off Adam when you come up the road, but we took you in and treated you like folks." She pulled her lips tight against her teeth. "I always say you got to live with 'em to know 'em—"

Jed could not let her go on.

"You ain't got no call to feel hard at me, Cannie."

"How come do we know you'll stay?"

"I told you I'd stay till October, till crops is in."

Seeing that Jed meant what he said, Basil let the anger go out of his voice.

"You aiming to go with him then, Jed?"

"I reckon."

"I wisht you wasn't. I hoped you'd stand in with me. Me and you make good hands together."

Jed looked at Basil and then at Cannie. They had a right to feel hard at him. They had given him a place to stay and made him one of the family. They had kept nothing from him. He had kept almost everything from them. He owed them more than saying he would stay and work out his time.

"It ain't that I've got anything agin you'uns, or your ways. It's something in me that won't let me stay—"

Cannie stopped him.

"I ain't taken in none by what you're saying. I see you going through the wish book and I said to myself, 'He ain't going to stay. He wants everything in the wish book, and he ain't going to get it staying here.' I been saying to Basil, 'You keep even with him on the money. Don't let him get into you none. He'll walk away just like he come.' "

She put her hand out to Basil.

"Let me hold on to the watch. How're we to know it wasn't stolen?"

"John'll tell you."

He thought of John somewhere up the road, too far to be called back. He shrank from the harshness in Basil's voice.

"Yeh, he'll tell us—in the fall. It'll be a long whet till he comes agin."

Cannie jerked her head up and down.

"What'll we do till then?" she asked.

"I cain't lose me no hand," Basil said. "I got too much work laid out to do it by myself." He looked across the cornfield. "Jed, you go on scaring the blackbirds away till sundown. Me and Cannie'll do some figgering on what we can expect out'n you, now that this has come up."

Cannie went toward the porch and then turned back.

"Jed, I ain't saying you took it, and I ain't saying you ain't, but I'll hide it in the clock for now. It ain't going to harm nobody to have it out o' sight till we know for sure."

Afraid to say anything else, Jed took the cane pole and walked slowly to the other end of the corn rows. He kept on walking back and forth, back and forth in the warm sun, unable to stop and rest, thinking as he went that if he walked this much on the road he would find John. He looked at Basil plowing in the next field. If he had not bounden himself to Basil, he would be walking on the road, traveling fast, trying to overtake John.

At dusk, when there were no more blackbirds in the sky, he went to the house. He passed close enough to the barn to hear Basil pulling down hay from the loft and shutting stall doors for the night. Times past, he would have waited for Basil and held the lot gate for him. This time he went alone and took the first turn at the wash pan and towel. The kitchen was dark and quiet. He went through the hall and to the fireplace room. It was lighted by a faint glow from coals on the hearth.

He stood in the door, listening to the steady ticking of the mantel clock. He could not see the face, but he knew how it looked and how the glass door opened for winding. The watch would be inside that door, lying next to the key. He listened, but, from where he stood, the ticking of the watch was drowned out by the clock. Still hearing no sound from the kitchen, he crept slowly toward the fireplace. When his hand touched the mantel he stopped. From there he heard the watch and the clock, like two pulses, one fast, the other slow.

"Jed, don't you set hand to that clock."

Cannie came in from the kitchen, breathing hard from stooping behind the door.

"Stand where you're caught," she said to Jed. "Basil, light a lamp. I'll show you what I said—once a thief, twice a thief."

"I ain't aiming to take it," he said. "I just wanted to hear it."

"Tell that to me and two or three others. We'll all believe you, won't we, Basil?"

"I reckon."

Cannie took the lamp and held it up by the clock. The watch lay beside the key.

"There it is, there it'll stay," she said. "Now you'uns go on to the table and I'll fix supper. Jed, Basil's got some thrashing out to do with you."

Cannie put supper on the table and the three of them sat down together. Jed looked from one to the other, trying to think of something to say to them. Their faces were grim. Basil did not try to make any jokes.

Cannie finished first and stacked her dishes in front of her.

"Now, Basil," she said, "get down to the settling."

"We ain't aiming to be hard on you, Jed," Basil said. "We could a turned you in but we ain't going to. We're taking a chance, not knowing you any better, but we'll let you stay. We want things to be like they was before till you work out your bounds. We won't hold you after that." He looked at Cannie and swallowed. "We ain't looking for no trouble, but it'll come if you step just once sideways crooked."

He said it without smiling. Jed looked at him and then down at his plate. He still had a slice of side meat and a piece of corn bread. He pushed his plate aside. He was not hungry.

Cannie looked past him.

"Basil," she said, "I ain't got no place but the clock to keep the watch."

"You don't need to hide it no more'n that. Jed wouldn't dast touch it, would you, Jed?"

Jed shook his head. No matter what they said, things would never be the same. They would look at him and worry about the watch. Before they left the table he knew he had to go find John. Only when he found John could he make them know he did not steal the watch. Then they could last it out together till October.

When they were not looking, he hid the side meat and corn bread under the bib of his overalls. It would have to do him till he found John. Then he went through the hall to the shed room, to wait till Basil and Cannie put out the light.

5

Past midnight, Jed walked steadily on, following the road up hill and down, feeling the wagon ruts under his feet, seeing not the dirt of the road but the opening between trees, a lighter darkness from the glow of the sky. His feet dragged, and he knew he had to stop and rest. Nobody can keep walking forever. Trouble was: he might rest and never find old John. Then he could never turn back—never square things with Basil and Cannie.

He did not know how many miles he had traveled. He knew only that he had started while the evening star still hung like a lantern in the treetops. Soon after supper, Basil and Cannie put out the lamp and went to bed. When he was sure they were asleep, he walked through the gate and up the road, with the clothes he had on and the pack of grub in his pocket.

He took off his shoes and kept on walking. Better to shiver from the chill earth than to give out too soon.

"Come morning, Basil'll miss me."

He thought of Basil going to the shed room, calling for him to get up and get going. Not till then would they know he had gone.

"He's gonna say to Cannie that I run off. Till I come back with some word from old John, they gonna say I just up and run off without'n a word. They gonna say how they took me in. They gonna say they could a turned me in and didn't. They gonna say how I got a-scared and run off. Then Basil'll listen to Cannie and take out after me."

Walking faster at the thought, he passed an open field and, far away, heard the sound of dogs barking. They had to be at somebody's house. He stopped to look, but it was too far off the road for him to see it. John could be sleeping at that house. He began to worry that he would pass John in the night and never find him. If he did not, he would never come back over this road. Basil and Cannie would have to think hard of him. He would never have to hear what they said or thought.

At a clearing in the woods, among treetops left by tiehackers, he built a fire and, when there was a warm place on the ground, lay down to sleep. Tired as he was, sleep did not come at once, and when it did, it brought no rest. In a kind of dream he kept on walking till there were shooting pains in his legs and a heaviness in his head.

At daylight, awakened by the twitter of blackbirds in the treetops, he went on the road again, holding a bite of corn bread in his mouth, tasting it as it turned sweet. A long line of blackbirds passed above him, enough to ruin Basil's corn, and him not there to scare them away. For the first time, he thought he had been wrong to go. He had bounden himself to Basil, to do whatever Basil wanted him to do, and he had taken Basil's money for the bounding. Basil had counted on him to see that the corn had a chance, and he had walked out . . . gone back on his word—something he had never done before. He had walked out, and Basil would have to send Cannie to do his work.

He looked back over the road he had traveled. He had gone too far to turn back, but he was no longer sure he should go ahead. What if he found John, and John cast him off for breaking his bounds? John would be in his rights not to take him along, knowing he had broken his bounds.

His steps were slower, and he stopped at times to look back down the road, half expecting to see Basil in the wagon, half hoping to see him. In broad daylight, what lay ahead seemed worse than anything he had left behind.

He heard the sound of a broadax striking a log and came to where a tiehacker was hewing out a railroad tie. Jed had never seen a railroad, but he had seen wagon loads of hand-hewn ties, mule-drawn, ox-drawn, on the way to the railroad siding at the edge of town.

The man, ready to swing, looked up and let the ax drop back to his shoulder.

"Howdy," Jed said, hoping to get past without questions.

The man set his ax in a gash in the log and stared at him.

"Howdy."

Jed kept walking.

"Hey, you lost something up the road?"

Jed paused.

"No, I ain't. I just come up from down the road a ways—"

"Running from something? You got the look o' running from something."

Jed turned and faced him.

"I come up the road looking for somebody. You seen a peddler a-passing this way?"

The tiehacker stooped down and with blue chalk redrew the marks on the end of the log he was hewing. Then he looked at Jed.

"I reckon I know who you mean. The old peddler. He passed that way in the e'ening when the sun was about a hand high. You hunting him?"

Jed started across a ditch to the road.

"I've got to find him."

"How come?"

Jed didn't have time to stand and talk. John might be at the next house, hitching up to go on.

"I've got something to tell him. He stayed with us night afore last, and I've got something to tell him. I've got to make haste so I won't miss him."

The tiehacker came close enough for Jed to get the souring smell of sweat and wood sap, and to see through his beard the whitish skin of a man who spent his days working in the shade of trees.

"Wait," he said. "I need you to help me a minute."

"What doing?"

"I cut a log and it fell where I cain't get at it. I'll give you a biscuit to help me get it out."

He took a biscuit out of a tin dinner bucket and Jed felt his mouth begin to water.

"Here."

Jed took the biscuit and saw that there were two logs, one fallen across the other. He put the biscuit in his pocket and, with a limb for a pry pole, helped the tiehacker roll one log to level ground. Too hungry to wait longer, Jed took a bite of the biscuit.

"Me and you'd make a good team," the tiehacker said. "I could use a good husky boy. I ain't got nothing but gal young'uns, and they ain't no good in the woods."

Without looking at Jed, he laid a shoulder to the second log. He strained till the back of his neck was red but the log did not move. He tried from the other end and then turned to Jed.

"I could make you my hand, if'n you ain't done nothing to be running from—if'n they ain't nobody after you."

Jed swallowed the last of the biscuit and brushed the flour from his mouth with the back of his hand.

"They ain't, but I cain't—"

"Aw, come on. Help me shove. I'll offer you a good bargain."

The log rocked but did not roll. The tiehacker tried swinging at it with his broadax. He could work one end but not the other.

"Wait," he said. "I'll get us the cant hook out'n the wagon. We'll roll it out all right."

Jed could not wait for him to get the cant hook. He could lose the whole day waiting. When the tiehacker was out of sight in the bushes Jed leaped the ditch to the road and started running. He heard a sound and, looking back, saw the tiehacker running along the ditch, the cant hook over his shoulder, a puzzled look on his face.

"Hey, wait," he yelled. "I want to ast you something."

Knowing what he would ask, Jed kept running.

"Hey, come back," the tiehacker yelled. "You et my biscuit. You ain't worked enough to pay for the biscuit you et."

He had dropped the cant hook and was running after Jed up the middle of the road.

"Stop, or I'll skin you alive."

Jed did not slow down. Catching had to come first, and he had made up his mind not to be caught—not by the tiehacker or Basil or anybody else. He ran faster, gaining on the tiehacker till he was out of sight around a bend in the road.

Winded, his eyes burning from sweat, he went on, letting his feet drag, but not letting them stop.

6

After noon, when he had passed around three more houses, Jed went down a long red clay hill, tired, hungry, talking to himself about how long he would have to go on before he could rest, afraid he was being followed on the road, afraid he would never catch sight of John's buggy around some bend.

Far down the road, where a stream passed under a culvert, he saw a man working alone with a shovel. He started toward the woods to go around him, only to see he was not a man but a colored boy close to his own age. Jed kept in the middle of the road and came close to him. From the way he smiled, Jed thought he must have seen him before down in the bottoms, in the fields picking or hoeing.

"What you doing?" Jed asked.

The boy stopped to lean on his shovel, his waist level with the road, his legs out of sight behind the bank of the culvert.

"Cleaning out the culvert so the water can dreen off."

"You seen a peddler go by?"

The boy wiped his face with his sleeve.

"I ain't remembering no peddler. He could a gone earlier."

"How long you been here?"

"They put me out here after dinner and left me to dig. Ain't nobody passed since then that I knows of. How come you wants the peddler?"

Jed wanted to talk to him. He was not one of the boys from the fields in the bottoms, but he sounded like them—low-voiced and friendly. Jed eased himself down on a patch of grass.

"I got something to ask of him. I been walking nigh on a day and night a-looking for him. I got to find him and ask him to take me with him." The boy leaned toward him, his eyes open wide, asking for more. "Some folks'd say I run off. I ain't run off. I had to get out. It was in me."

The boy jerked his head back.

"Then you better keep on a-going. Don't let none o' them see you."

Jed looked at the boy, standing stock still beside the culvert, his feet and legs hidden. He swallowed hard and wiped again at his face with his sleeve.

"I'd go with you if'n I could."

"What's holding you?"

"Ain't you knowed?"

The boy moved his feet and a chain rattled. Jed looked over the bank and saw the chains on the boy's ankles and the heavy iron ball by his feet. The chain gang—

"You on the chain gang?"

"You looking at me, ain't you?"

"I know, but I ain't never seen nobody on the chain gang—just heard tell of it. What'd you do?"

The boy gave a quick look up the road.

"Same as you. I run off. I run off and they caught me and put me on the chain gang."

"That's nothing wrong—"

"It ain't that I run off from home. I reckon they wouldn't a cared if'n I'd a went from here to Jericho and back. I got hungry and had to have me some grub, so I passed by a tater field and took me some taters. I was grabbling them out of the ground and got caught. They give me sixty days—"

"Sixty days?"

"Sixty days and costs. It's about over. I ain't kept count, but it cain't be long. Joe says he'll keep track o' time for me."

"Joe?"

"Yeh, Joe. We got two trusties. Joe and Peavey."

Jed began to feel uneasy.

"You got that many on the chain gang?"

The boy laughed.

"Man, we got them stretched out three miles up the road, all like me, doing time. When I get out I'm going back home, where no trusty'll ever get a-holt o' me agin."

"How come you run off in the first place?"

"I didn't see nothing to stay for, so I went. It ain't that they didn't talk to me about trouble. They did, but I ain't had time to listen."

Jed knelt on the culvert close to him.

"My name's Jed. What's yours?"

"Luster. I ain't never been called nothing else."

Jed repeated the name and then went to the middle of the road.

"Where you going?" Luster asked.

"On up the road."

"You better look out for Peavey. He's the trusty on horseback. He'd as soon turn you in as look at you. If'n I was you, I'd walk around Peavey. He ain't nobody to fool with. It's woods a long ways on both sides o' the road."

Luster took his shovel and started digging at the mud. Without looking back, Jed went down through the borrow ditch and hid himself in low-growing bushes that had already turned green with spring. Keeping the opening of the road in sight, he kept on going.

His steps grew slower and slower. His feet bogged in the soft earth. Thorns of stretchberry vines pulled his clothes. But he was afraid of the road, and of Peavey. He believed every word Luster had said about Peavey. He'd be a fool to go anywhere close to Peavey.

7

Luster had said the chain gang was stretched out three miles up the road. Jed kept to the bushes, out of sight, a good three miles, and then at least another mile to make certain he had walked around the chain gang and Peavey. The day, already shortening, seemed to go faster in the thickets, and he felt more alone—not lost but alone, with nothing to do but keep on going, through the day, and as far as he could into the night.

When the sun was getting low he came to a creek that, muddy and deep, forced him back to the road, to cross by a bridge on the road. Slowly he worked his way through a fringe of bushes and climbed up from the borrow ditch to the graded shoulder of the road. The bridge was ahead of him, a plank bridge with handhewn banisters heavy and dark. He listened to the hollow sound of his shoes on the planks, but his eyes were on the road, on a bend in the road far ahead. He could make it around that bend. Then he would have to stop and rest. He looked ahead, and forgot to look behind.

He heard a horse coming at a gallop and looked back. A white man was in the saddle, whipping the horse with a white felt hat. Peavey. The trusty on horseback. Jed crossed a culvert and started running for the woods, but the horse's hoofs were close on him before he could get down to the borrow ditch. He stopped, but did not look around.

"Where you going, bub?" the man asked. "What you up to?"

"Nothing."

"How come you're afraid to be seen on the public road?"

"I—"

"You running from something?"

"No—"

"Not much you ain't. I seen you a-talking to Luster. Maybe you don't know it's agin the law to talk to a convict. Maybe you do. Maybe you're up to something, talking to him."

Jed shook his head and edged closer to the borrow ditch. Across it the bushes grew thick.

"Where you think you're going?" the man yelled.

He turned the horse in front of Jed, forcing him to stop, and dropped down to the ditch, facing him. Jed looked at the thin dark face, the dull dark eyes, and knew better than to tell him anything.

"Up the road a ways."

"My name's Peavey. I don't take lying from nobody. Where you come from?"

"Down the road a ways."

"You run off from home?"

"No—"

"I reckon that's it. You run off from home, and in no time a-tall you taken up with Luster. He run off from home, too, and got caught stealing. You steal something?"

"No, sir."

"It mostly goes that way. A boy wants to go off on his own, so he steals somebody's stuff and takes off. I've seen it a thousand times. If I was to take you back where you come from, would they tell me you ain't stoled nothing?"

Jed heard the question and braced himself to leap. He knew what would happen. Basil and Cannie would tell him about the watch and he would be put on the chain gang. He jumped the borrow ditches and headed for the bushes.

"Come back here."

Jed heard Peavey running behind him and felt his hands on his overall straps. Unable to jerk loose, he had to stop.

"How come you run?" Peavey demanded. "You must a been guilty. Ain't nobody gonna run like that unless'n he's guilty. Come clean now. What'd you do?"

"I told you. I ain't done nothing."

"You said it, and I ain't a-believing you. You done something all right. It shows in your face."

Jed thought of old John, going farther and farther up the road, taking with him the answers to Peavey's questions.

"I ain't done nothing," he said. "Cain't you let me go? I've got to go. I swear not to come back this way."

Peavey stared at him and shook his head. Then he got on his horse and pulled the reins tight.

"By my lights, holding's easier'n catching, so I'll hold on to you till I get word from the Cap'n. He's the law—no two ways about it. He's back down the road somewheres, watching the scrapers or fresnos. Me and you'll march along till we find him. I'll tell him what I know about you. If he looks at you and says, 'You c'n git,' for all of me you c'n git, but not till he says it."

What he meant was that Jed would walk and he would follow behind on his horse. Turned back on the road, Jed knew he would never find John. He let his shoulders slump and his feet drag. Peavey stopped from time to time to look at the road work, or to speak to a pick or shovel man bound to the earth by ball and chains. Where the road had been graded, it was soft like fresh-plowed ground. They passed the plow crew, with mules and plows turning up the clayey earth, followed by the scrapers—one man, one mule, one scraper to a team, with another man to set the scraper, deep or shallow. Near sundown they came to the fresnos, pulled by four mules, big enough to haul a wagon load of dirt.

Jed looked at the men as he passed. Convicts. He had never seen a convict before Luster. He had never seen white men and colored men working together the way they did on the chain gang. It was close to quitting time, but they worked as if there would never be a quitting time.

The Cap'n was watching the fresnos, sitting in his buggy with a hound dog lying at his feet. He was a big man, red of hair, red of face. There was a rusty redness in his leather jacket and Stetson hat, and in the rifle scabbard propped against the dashboard.

He leaned on the arm rest and looked down at Jed.

"What you got there, Peavey?" he asked.

"Might be one thing, might be another. I'm still trying to find out. He says his name is Jed. He says he come from down the road a-piece, but he ain't named no place. I ast him questions, but I ain't found out nothing about him for sure. All I can say is, I ain't trusting nobody who runs when you look at him."

Jed looked up at the Cap'n's heavy face, at his eyes blue and small in the heavy folds of his lids. He knew he would have to tell the Cap'n what he had told Peavey.

"I ain't done nothing. I was just a-walking on the road. That ain't no harm to nobody, walking on the road—

Peavey stopped him.

"I seen what I seen, Cap'n. He was talking to Luster, like he was used to talking to Luster. When he went on he didn't stick to the public road, like he was a-scared to stick to the public road. I watched him and come up on him and he run. You cain't tell me he ain't done nothing."

"You ain't got much on him, Peavey."

"It don't take much when you seen what I seen."

The Cap'n took a long hard look at Jed.

"What'll we do with him, Peavey?"

Jed knew now that he was caught. Peavey had turned him in, and the Cap'n was not ready to let him go.

"I say hold him. Like as not, if we hold him long enough somebody'll come along looking for him, and be mighty glad we helt him. He could tell you who right now, if'n he wanted to talk."

Without thinking, Jed looked back along the road. It could be the tiehacker. It could be Basil, coming in the wagon to take him back to his bounding.

Peavey's voice rose, high and shrill.

"You seen him, Cap'n. You seen him look down the road like he was a-feared of what he would see."

The Cap'n turned from Jed to Peavey.

"Looks like you've got something there, Peavey."

It was enough for them to hold him, and he was afraid to say another word to them.

The Cap'n held his hand up to the sun.

"Quitting time, Peavey," he said. "You can tell the men to knock off for the night." He looked at Jed. "He can pile in the wagon with the pick and shovel men. Tell Joe to keep an eye on him to camp. We don't want to have to go beating the bushes for him."

When Peavey yelled quitting time, the men unhitched their teams and, leaving their scrapers and plows and fresnos in the dirt, climbed on mules' backs and, with a rattling of trace chains, started a ragged line up the road. A wagon driven by a Negro trusty followed them, stopping for pick and shovel men to climb up over the sideboards with their balls and chains.

At a word from Peavey, he stopped and Jed climbed in. Peavey went to the head of the line. The wagon Jed was in came near the end, with some men on muleback behind it and then the Cap'n, with the hound dog on the seat beside him.

Jed, squeezed in by the endgate, saw Luster with his back propped against the spring seat. Between them were five Negroes and one sallow-faced white man. They looked at Jed's ankles and then at his face.

"You got some smoking?" a Negro asked him.

"No, I ain't. I ain't never smoked."

Another one leaned toward him.

"You got any dipping? I could sho use me some good Levi Garrett."

"No."

"No baccy. No snuff. What is you got?"

"Nothing a-tall."

"Nothing to buy it with?"

Just as he was going to say *nothing*, he felt hands going through his pockets. He knew they would find nothing, not even a piece of corn bread. He shrank under the touch of the hands, afraid of what they would do to him because he had nothing for them.

They saw him and laughed.

"Hey, Joe," one of the men called up to the trusty. "Don't worry none about us taking what he's got. He ain't got nothing to take."

Then they left him alone.

8

While the sun was still a red glow through the trees, they turned off the road, passed an old farmhouse where the Cap'n lived and the muddy yellow tent of the convicts, and came to a pasture that had been made into a barbed-wire corral for the mules. The Cap'n stopped at his door and took his gun and dog inside with him. Peavey sat on his horse at the gate, counting the men and mules as they went past. When he got down from the wagon, Jed was far from the road—so far that he could not see where it wound up the red clay hills. Peavey was between him and the road, Peavey and the eight-strand barbed-wire fence.

"Unhitch."

Peavey's voice rose above the sounds of chains and men.

"Kitchen men! Hit the kitchen."

Half a dozen men started toward the tent, hobbling along, dragging the heavy balls forward first with one foot, then the other.

"Mule skinners—"

Peavey stopped and waited till the kitchen men were looking back.

"Skin them mules."

There was laughing and grumbling, and the shuddering of hides as the mules shook themselves free of their harness.

"All you other peapickers. You know what jobs you got. Make haste. Cut the wood. Haul the water. Clean up what's got to be cleaned up. I don't want to see nobody slacking off, and I ain't standing for no jawing. Shake a leg now. You, too, Joe."

The trusty called Joe climbed down from the spring seat, looking bigger on his feet, darker in the dusk.

"Peavey act like the boss man," a man said to him in a low voice. "How come he act like the boss man?"

Joe looked at Peavey sitting high on his horse.

"How many times you gonna ast me that? I done tole you. He been a trusty so long he ain't know nothing else. I say, when a man done done his time, he better hit the road, trusty or no trusty. Me, when I get out, I'll go so fast I'll burn the road."

"Why don't you tell that to Peavey?"

"Ain't no use. He's got a horse to ride and men to boss. He ain't gonna git that nowheres but on the chain gang."

Peavey rode across the corral and saw Jed and Luster standing near the wagon, waiting to be told what to do.

"Hey, you two," he yelled. "How long you aiming to stand there with your hands in your pockets? Pick you up some blocks o' hay and start scattering it out'n the pasture. Put it on the clean spots where the mules ain't tromped up no mud. Keep a-hustling till it's all put out."

The clean spots were down the corral from the wagons, on a rim of hill not far from the woods. Jed made three trips to Luster's one and, when they were alone, told him to take it slow, bound as he was with the ball and chain. He hated to see Luster hitching along, up hill and down. He had been bounden, but never like Luster.

The last load took them under the rim of the hill. When the hay was scattered, Luster stood looking into the thick woods, still light in the gray treetops but dark along the ground. He touched Jed on the shoulder and pointed to a black line of trees.

"They's a slough in there."

"How do you know?"

"I done seen it. They sent me out a-chasing a mule and I seen it." He brought his hand down to his thigh. "Tonight me an' you gonna wade that slough."

Jed looked at his eyes, wide, white against his dark skin.

"What're you talking about?"

"Running off."

"Running off?"

"Nothing else but. You set me to thinking how long I been here. I ain't kept count, but I been here from tater time to planting time. That's more'n sixty days and costs. Peavey ain't said I could go, but Peavey ain't a-gonna see me in the dark. He ain't about to see you neither, if'n we do it right."

He laughed and slapped Jed on the back.

"They don't know it, but me an' you done made for night traveling."

He looked at the woods again and Jed knew he meant to go there when it was night. Luster was right to go. He had done enough time for grabbling somebody else's potatoes. But he was not like Luster. There was nothing for him to do time for. He had been turned in, but nothing else.

Luster started up the hill.

"Come on. We gotta get to the tent ahead o' Peavey."

Halfway up the hill Jed found a piece of haywire and hooked it to the ball. Walking close to Luster, he lifted it so that Luster had the hobble but not the weight.

"That cinches it," Luster said. "Me an' you made to travel double."

"I don't know. I don't have nothing to run off for."

Luster stopped.

"You will have. Mark my word. Peavey'll come up with something. You'll see we got to go together."

They crossed the corral and when they were near the wagons Luster stooped down and took off the wire.

"No need'n letting Peavey see this," he said. "You better hold on to the wire."

Jed bent the wire into small loops and put it inside the bib of his overalls. Then they passed Peavey, waiting to lock the corral gate.

It was good dark when they came to the cooking fires between the Cap'n's house and the tent. The kitchen men were ready to dish up. Pick and shovel men, scraper men, fresno men all waited in line, all of them with their feet bound by balls and chains. They shuffled past a table, not talking, but rattling their chains as they went. Jed, coming last, took the tin plate, tin cup, tin fork handed him. When he came to the end of the line he had a plate of red beans, a piece of corn bread, and a cup of black coffee.

"Same grub we had yistiddy," Luster said. "And the day before. Good thing it's so dark we cain't see what we eating."

To Jed, it was grub, and he was hungry. He thought of a joke Basil sometimes made to Cannie, and said it to Luster, trying to make himself sound like Basil.

"I cain't complain about it. I ain't et in so long my stomach thinks my throat's cut."

Luster did not laugh.

"You better swallow what you going to," he said.

They ate fast, standing near the tent, part of a group of men silent except for the sound of tin forks on tin plates. Then they fell in line again and washed their plates and cups in a kettle over a fire.

It was Joe's turn to keep count of the men. As they washed up, he looked at their faces and let them go to the open flap of the tent.

He kept Jed beside him till the others had gone in. Then he gave him a metal cot and blanket.

"It looks full in there," he said, "but we always got room for one more. Set up anywheres you wants to."

The tent was long and low, suspended on three poles, murky with the light of coal-oil lanterns, rank with the smell of men who worked all day in the dirt and slept in their clothes. The tent walls were down to keep out the chill of the night, and a fire burned in an oil-drum stove. Jed looked down the two rows of cots at the men, black men and white men mixed in together, sitting down, lying down, not talking, not doing anything but resting. Nothing else to do.

Nothing for Jed to do but rest with them, and wait for the night to pass. He saw Luster at the back of the tent and went toward him. Luster pushed his cot to one side to make a space for Jed between him and the tent wall. Luster said nothing, but Jed knew what he meant. With one hand he could push the canvas up and be outside in the darkness. He set up the cot and spread the blanket. He sat down and looked at Luster, stretched out on his cot, the ball lying beside his feet. Jed swallowed hard.

"I never been in a place like this before," he said. "I ain't never laid down by a colored boy."

He was going to say *by a nigger* the way everybody on the chain gang said it, but could not. He saw the look on Luster's face and was glad he hadn't.

"I ain't aiming to harm you none," Luster said. "You ain't got no need to be a-scaid o' me. I'm a convict and I'm black, but it ain't gonna rub off on you none."

Joe came through the tent flap with some loops of chain over his shoulder and a pair of handcuffs in his hand. He counted again to see that all the men were there and started down the rows of cots.

"Set for the night?" he asked a Negro convict.

The man stretched out on the cot and Joe looped a chain through the chain on his ankles and locked him to the cot.

"Them that's run off before gits locked up like that," Luster whispered to Jed. "You ain't needing to worry none. You ain't done nothing to be locked up for." He winked once. "When they find out you cain't be trusted to stay, you'll done be gone for good."

Joe came to a thin-faced white man in blue duckings and jumper. He looked tired and cold and beat. Dirt from the road reddened the whiskers around his mouth. Without a word, he stretched out on his cot and lay still while Joe locked his feet to the cot.

Joe passed down the aisle from his cot and, without looking back, began singing.

"If I had my druthers,. .
I'll tell you if I can,
I'd druther be a nigger
Than a po' white man."

The man turned his head away and covered his face with his

blanket. Negroes near him lifted up their heads and laughed. The white men the length of the tent lay silent, not moving. Jed looked at their faces and then at Joe, standing big and tall over them.

"How come he sung that?" Jed asked Luster.

"To keep them under. It's less trouble for a trusty to keep them under."

"How come they let him get away with it?"

"They got on chains. He ain't. How they gonna stop him? They know when they under."

"How come Peavey don't stop him? Or the Cap'n?"

"Peavey ain't come to the tent yet, is he?"

"No."

"You ain't seen the Cap'n here?"

"No."

"Who's the boss here now?"

"It looks like Joe."

"That's how they work it. When they not here, Joe's the boss. You cain't blame him letting people know it. Right now the Cap'n's taking his comfort somewheres else. So's Peavey. Joe do be rough on the white men when they ain't around. He dast not let them catch him at it. They'd take about two minutes to whittle him down."

Trembling, Jed watched Joe come toward his cot. He was grinning and humming the tune under his breath. He stopped and stood swinging a pair of handcuffs around his finger.

"What's yo' name agin?" he asked.

"Jed."

"Now, look here, Jed. You seen enough to know who's boss around here. You know I ain't taking no lip."

He waited for Jed to speak.

"Yes."

"The Cap'n's coming to the tent tonight. When he comes, I want you to look peart, 'n' not have no sass. You ain't got on no bracelets now, but I got these handy. You step outa line, I'll snap 'em on. You hear me?"

"Yes."

"You better."

Joe went back down the tent and sat on a bench near the stove. Luster waited for the hum of voices to rise again. Then he whispered to Jed, leaning over without rattling his chains.

"You seen how mean he can be?"

"Yes."

"Now you ready to go?"

Jed answered from a dry throat.

"Any time you say."

"I say tonight. You better wrop up in yo' blanket and take some rest so's we can travel fast. I'll watch out to see you don't get in no trouble sleeping."

9

Jed felt a hand on his shoulder and shut his eyes against the light when the blanket was pulled from over his head.

"Better wake up," Luster said. "Cap'n's coming this way any minute now. It ain't a-gonna please him none if'n he finds you asleep. He git man mad."

Jed sat up and looked down the tent. The men were all sitting up on their cots, facing the open tent flap, waiting. The fire had been built up and the sides of the stove glowed red. Joe stood straight and still, facing the flap, with his back to the stove. From their looks, Jed knew Luster had waited to the last minute to wake him.

"Here come the Cap'n," Joe yelled.

Peavey came first and, with a rattle of chains, the men not bound to their cots rose to their feet. The Cap'n, with his dog at his heels, came next, looking bigger and bulkier in the shadowy light. He took a chair by the stove and the red light warmed his face to a brighter red. When the dog had settled at his feet, he cut himself a plug of chewing tobacco and motioned for the men to sit down. He held up a boot crusted with red mud.

"Where's my shine?" he asked.

"Here I is, Cap'n."

A dark little man in blue overalls and a dirty white shirt dragged his ball and chains over to the Cap'n's chair. On his knees, the boot in his lap, he began scraping away the mud with a wooden paddle.

The Cap'n looked at the men and then at Peavey.

"How about it, Peavey?" he asked. "You got any show for me tonight?"

Peavey turned to Joe.

"What you say, Joe? You think the boys is rested enough to knock up a little tune for the Cap'n?"

That's how it is, Jed thought. The Cap'n talks to Peavey, and Peavey talks to Joe—the talk going down. He looked at the white man, chained to his cot, lying down, his face turned away. Talk going down, but not coming back up the same way. Nobody telling the Cap'n on Joe.

Joe let his teeth show white at Peavey.

"Sho can. They raring to go."

"Then get them going."

Joe walked down between the row of cots and back again to the middle tent pole. Facing the Cap'n he leaned against it and held out his hands, with the pinkish brown palms up. He closed his eyes and hummed a tune. Once through, and, at a nod from him, the men began humming with him. He held a hand to his ear, listening, and, marking time with his foot, went from humming to singing.

"Oh, Lawdy, oh, Lawd."

His voice was soft and deep and full of trouble.

"Oh, Lawdy, oh, Lawd."

At the sound of the men singing the words Jed felt a tingling rise up his backbone and spread through his shoulders. It was not like Cannie singing alto. It was like a whole singing school, but better—like down in the bottoms—like the moaning low he heard in the cotton fields nigh on sunset when the hoe hands looked to the end of the row and rest.

"I'm on the chain gang now."
"I'm on the chain gang now."
"Oh, Lawdy, oh, Lawd."
"Oh, Lawdy, oh, Lawd."
"Cain't you tell me how?"
"Cain't you tell me how?"

As they sang, the Cap'n leaned forward in his chair, catching the warmth of the fire on his hands. The shine slapped polish on his boots, his fingers keeping time with Joe's heavy foot.

> "*Oh, Lawdy, oh, Lawd.*"
> "Oh, Lawdy, oh, Lawd."
> "*I gotta get off.*"
> "I gotta get off."

Joe raised his hands and brought them down in a loud crack.

> "*I want somebody, oh, Lawd,*
> *Just to tell me how.*"

The Cap'n stopped the singing and pointed a finger at Joe.

"That's enough o' that'n. What you want? Everybody picking up and walking out on me?"

Joe laughed.

"They ain't about to go nowheres, Cap'n. Look at their foots."

The Cap'n smiled and the men settled back on their cots.

"I'd as lief have some jigging. Got any new dancers, Joe?"

Joe shook his head.

"You ain't brought me none, is you?"

The Cap'n slapped his leg.

"Not lately. Not much luck lately. What do you have?"

"We still got old Slim. You want old Slim?"

"Reckon he'll have to do."

At a nod from Joe, two convicts brought two wide boards and laid them in the aisle. A tall, slow-moving Negro got up from his cot and dragged his ball and chains to the boards. A white man began knocking a slow rhythm with a pair of bones. Slim began swaying his hips.

"Lift off his burden, Joe," a man down the aisle yelled. "He ain't gonna dance none in that fix. You gotta stoop a-down and loosen his foots."

Joe stooped down and unlocked the chains. Slim kicked the

ball aside and tested the boards with his toe. He swung his arms and then his legs.

"The bones is a-knocking, Slim," Joe yelled. "Limber up and let 'er go."

Jed, on the edge of his cot, watched Slim dance down the boards and back. Then he watched Slim's shadow dancing on the tent wall, in whirling, changing patterns of flailing arms, stilt-like legs. He heard the knock of bones, the rap of work shoes on the loose boards. Joe started a humming that was low at first and then louder, faster. The men sang and yelled and clapped their hands, free but for the chains that bound their feet. Slim danced faster and faster and, out of breath at last, fell on his cot, his feet stretched out still for the chains. The humming trailed away and broke off to silence. Joe snapped the lock and leaned against the tent pole. The men slumped back on their cots.

When the tent was still, the Cap'n looked at Peavey.

"Where's our new boy? he asked. "He ought to be good for a laugh or two, green as he is."

"Bring him up, Joe," Peavey said. "Bring up Jed. See can he make a laugh for the Cap'n."

Jed looked at Luster.

"I cain't do nothing—"

"You got to. They ain't gonna let up till you does. You ain't got no leg bracelets now. You don't do what they say, you'll be wearing them."

Feeling the eyes of the men on him, Jed put on his shoes and walked up the tent to the boards. With his hands at his sides he stood facing the Cap'n. Peavey nodded to him and then to Joe.

"Can you sing us a song?" Joe asked.

"No, I ain't never."

"Can you dance?"

"No."

"What can you do to pleasure the Cap'n?"

Jed looked at the Cap'n, trying to make him understand that there was nothing he could do—that he did not want to make a laugh for anybody. The Cap'n only stared at him, waiting.

Jed felt the water in his mouth.

"I don't know nothing I can do."

The Cap'n gave Joe a quick look.

"The Cap'n says to learn you something," Joe said. "It ain't gonna hurt you none to make a laugh for the Cap'n. You ready to learn something?"

Jed rubbed his sleeve across his face.

"I reckon, if you want."

Joe grinned and pointed down the tent.

"Look at this tent, full o' convicts, doing their time. It looks like church, but it sho God ain't church, 'n' I'll tell you why. The Lawd's got a mighty big heaven—big enough to hold all the sinners in the world, once they gits saved. The Cap'n ain't got no church, no heaven, but he's got this great big tent full o' sinners doing their time to git cleaned up. He's all the time wanting people to come to his tent and git cleaned up. Luster, you come here. We got to show Jed what we mean. Come on, Luster. Don't be so slow."

Luster got up and, with a rattling of chains, came slowly up between the rows of cots. When he was on the boards Joe held up a hand and he stopped.

"How come you here, Luster?" Joe asked. "Tell us how you made it to the Cap'n's tent?"

Luster looked down at his feet.

"I stoled."

"Stoled what?"

"Taters."

The other convicts began to laugh.

"Nothing but taters."

When the Cap'n smiled, Joe pointed a finger at Luster and began singing. The man with the bones took up the beat.

"Tater stealer, don't stay away,
Tater stealer, don't stay away. . . . ."

He clapped his hands and raised his arms. "Come on now. Everybody sing."

"Our Cap'n say they's room enough,
Room enough in the tent for us all,
Our Cap'n say they's room enough,
Don't stay away."

Joe looked at Luster.

"You singing, Luster?"

"I singing."

"Sing it agin on your lonesome. Let the Cap'n hear you, so's you won't ever forgit."

With his head down, Luster mumbled through the words. Then, without looking up, he went back to his cot and sat down.

Joe turned to Jed.

"Now you see how it's done, we'll sing it for you. What brand o' sinning did you do?"

Jed looked at Peavey and the Cap'n.

"I told them I ain't done nothing."

Joe shook his head.

"Everybody's done something. You've got to've done something to get in this tent."

Jed thought of the watch. He thought of Basil standing in the yard holding it in his hand. *I didn't steal it. John'll tell you I didn't steal it.*

"I ain't stole nothing."

Joe looked about ready to believe him.

"I ain't said you stoled."

He took a step toward Peavey.

"You turned him in, Peavey. What was he a-doing to make you turn him in? I got to have something solid."

"A-hoofing it down that old red road like running from the devil—"

Joe slapped his leg and began to laugh.

"I ain't never met up with one like that'n," he said. "I don't know how to put it in a song, but I'll have me a whang at it."

He closed his eyes and set the beat with his hand. He hummed the tune through once, and then again. With a jerk of his head he opened his eyes and began singing.

> "*Red road hoofer, don't stay away,*
> *Red road hoofer, don't stay away—*"

He stopped singing and dropped his hands to his sides.

"It ain't no use, Cap'n. I cain't git me no feeling outa something like that—not when we got a tent full o' crap shooters, wife beaters, moonshiners—nigh about anything you'd want to h'ist a tune on. Nobody c'n git worked up over a white boy hoofing it along a public road."

He gave Peavey a sharp look.

"Unless'n it's Peavey. He gits worked up easy. You want Peavey to try to git some fun out'n him, Cap'n?"

The Cap'n shook his head.

"I don't cotton too much to Peavey's kind o' fun."

He looked at Peavey and frowned.

"If'n we're down to that, the show's over."

With a motion of his hand to show he meant what he said, he got up and started toward the tent flap, with his dog close beside him. Joe went past Peavey, who was hanging back, shamefaced.

"Cap'n?" Joe called.

The Cap'n turned back.

"Peavey ain't told me how long you keeping that boy."

"Ain't nobody said yet. Peavey wants to keep on holding him, but I don't know. I'd as lief let him go at daylight."

The Cap'n came toward Jed.

"C'n you hit the road by daylight?"

Jed thought of John, on the road up ahead, or taking the road north to the ferry. He could get in some good walking before daylight.

"Sooner, if you'd let me. Right now, if'n you want it."

The Cap'n shook his head and jerked a thumb at Peavey.

"Send him packing at daylight if they ain't nobody looking for him."

Peavey nodded and went to the tent flap to hold it open. The Cap'n whistled to his dog and started out.

"Cap'n," Joe said. "C'n I say something, Cap'n?"

The Cap'n stopped, half-hidden by the tent flap.

"I don't know how come you cain't."

"Cap'n, you been wanting a good white boy to do for you. I been watching this'n. He ain't far from what you been looking for."

"I don't know about holding him."

Peavey's voice was high and flat.

"He c'n be helt, Cap'n. He ain't running from nothing. Like I said, you look back down the road a ways. Somebody'll tell you how come he's running."

Jed could not see the Cap'n's face when he spoke.

"Hold him till morning. I been needing a boy like him all right."

Peavey waited till the Cap'n was out of hearing.

"Lights out, Joe," he said, "and I don't want no more of your lip."

He let the tent flap drop behind him.

Back at his cot, Jed watched Luster lift his ball and chains and rest them beside his feet. At daylight he would be called by the Cap'n but not Luster. The Cap'n might let him go, but not Luster. When the lights were out, he sat on the edge of his cot, thinking of what to do about Luster. After a time he heard Luster whisper.

"You backing out on me, Jed? You gonna go on and leave me here?"

"I ain't said so."

"It'd be easy."

Jed lay still in the darkness, trying to think what to answer. The Cap'n had said he could go at daylight. He had no call to run off with Luster when he would be on his own at daylight.

"I know what you thinking," Luster said. "You thinking the Cap'n gonna let you go easy. It ain't the Cap'n. It's Peavey. He'll scratch around till he finds something agin you. You'll be helt, like he said. He meant it, what he said about looking back down the road."

Not far to look, Jed thought. A man on horseback could get back to Basil and Cannie in no time.

"What you saying, Jed?" Luster whispered. "I got to know now. You an' me traveling together like we said?"

He heard Luster breathing. He heard a clink of chains as he sat up. He knew that if he went with Luster he would lose his chance to find old John. He thought of Peavey and knew he had to go with Luster. He leaned as far as he could toward him.

"We'll hit the road any time you say."

10

Jed felt Luster's hand on his shoulder and knew it was time to go. He lifted himself up on the cot and waited, listening to the breathing of sleeping men, till he was sure Luster had worked his way outside the tent wall. He heard no clink of chain, no sound of movement, but he knew when Luster had gone ahead of him. Moving slowly, trembling with night chill, he eased himself down from the steel springs of the cot to the ground next to the tent wall. Then he rolled under the canvas and bumped into Luster, kneeling on the ground waiting for him.

Afraid to whisper, he took the haywire from his overalls and ran his hands down Luster's legs till he came to the chains. Luster had wrapped them with rags to keep them from clinking. He found the ring on the ball and hooked the wire to it. When he lifted the ball, Luster stood up and they started with slow steps through the darkness.

Without a word between them, they came to the barbed-wire fence of the corral and rolled under it. Jed heard the mules grazing on hay, and the sound of hoof-slaps on the ground.

"It'd be easier to follow the line of the fence," he whispered.

"We cain't," Luster said. "We got to go through the mules. Ain't nobody gonna hear us if we go through the mules. They gonna tromp up our tracks. Daylight comes, they cain't tell we left by the pasture. You step where the mules is been, you ain't gonna leave no smell."

With Luster in the lead, they went through the mules, passing close enough to hear their breathing, to feel the warmth from their bodies, careful not to touch them, or make a sound that would start a stampede.

They reached the rim of the hill before they took time for a breath, or for a look at the sky, bright with stars, or at the heavy darkness of the woods. Jed picked out the pointer stars of the Dipper, and then the North Star. If he went to the right of the North Star and kept going, he would hit the road back to Basil and Cannie. He began to wish he could go back now, to set his feet under their table, to sleep in the shed room. He could go, but he could not take Luster. They would have no room for Luster.

"We got to hit the slough," Luster said. "It starts a little past where the woods begins."

"We have to go by the slough? It'll slow us down a heap going that way."

Luster would not be changed.

"I been here a long time," he said. "I seen 'em come. I seen 'em go. Them that's stayed gone went by the slough."

Moving slowly, away from the mules, they went down the hill and under the barbed-wire fence. Bushes at the beginning of the woods made a wall that they had to push and crawl through. They lost time, and Jed began to worry that daylight would catch them before they were out of sight of the camp. When he thought they should try another way, the bushes thinned out under big gum trees and they came to the slough. They could see the black water and the reflections of stars in it. Luster crept to the edge.

"Us wading in," he said.

"How come?" Jed asked, thinking of the wetness and the chill. "We gonna be wet. We cain't go so fast wet."

Luster grabbed his arm.

"We got to wash off the scent. Ain't you seen that hound? Ain't you seen the Cap'n's hound? That's the bloodhound he keeps to track down anybody that tries to run off."

Jed had seen the hound.

"Looks like a pot-licking dog to me."

Luster leaned toward the water.

"He's pure bloodhound. You c'n tell by the droop-down ears. He may a looked like a pot licker, but he ain't when he gits on the trail of a convict. I tell you, they ain't nothing to do but hit the water."

Luster waded in first and Jed, still holding up the ball, came after him. He felt the water rise cold as ice to his knees. He felt his shoes sink in the muddy bottom, pulling him down when he wanted to go faster. Bloodhound. Luster should have told him it was a bloodhound. He began to blame Luster for not telling him. Nobody could go fast enough to outrun a bloodhound. It was too late to turn back—too late for anything but keeping on wading the slough.

"I told you the slough'd be slow going," he said.

"Ain't nothing else that'll get shet o' the scent."

Slowly they moved along the slough, keeping in the shallow water near the edge, with Luster going ahead, pushing the branches that came out over the water, holding them back for Jed. Jed carried the ball, with arms aching and fingers burning from the cut of the wire. He wanted to stop for a rest, but Luster kept pushing on.

"It's gonna be day in no time," he said. "They gonna see our cots and know we done gone. We dassent let 'em catch us running off. We dassent ever let Peavey catch us. We got to stick it out to the end o' the slough and make ourselves travel faster on dry land."

When Jed thought he would drop, they waded out of the water and through a boggy swamp. In thick woods along a ridge they lay down on the ground to catch their breath before going on. Luster found the North Star, pale now in the brightening sky.

"We'll set to the left o' that," he said. "We'll set a right smart to the left and keep on a-walking. We keep walking long enough, we gonna come to the river and it won't be no trouble a-tall to find the ferry."

Jed sat up.

"The ferry?"

Long ago old John had said he would go north by the ferry.

"I said the ferry." Luster's voice was sharp and then softer. "I reckon I ain't told you I come across on the ferry. When I run off

I took the road to the south and come to the ferry. It costs a nickel to cross a-foot, but I ain't had the nickel, so the ferryman let me help him pull the rope. I didn't mind working, being as it was taking me where I wanted to go. I come across an' I seen more'n I wanted to see. I'll pull the rope twice as hard to take me back."

After a moment of silence, he laughed in his throat.

"I c'n tell you how it's gonna be," he said. "Come daylight, me an' you gonna get shet o' this burden and travel fast. We gonna come to the ferry and the man'll let us pull the rope. We gonna cross over faster'n he ever went. It's only a ways up the road from the ferry to my house. We git there, we gonna eat and sleep. Man, how we gonna eat and sleep. It'll take me a month o' Sundays to git caught up."

Jed saw clearly for Luster, but not for himself.

"Where do we go after that?" he asked.

"Me? I ain't a-going nowheres. I done had my belly full o' running off. I'd as lief stay put till somebody moves me."

Jed could not think what he would do, but he knew he would not stay with Luster. He'd as well be bounden to Basil as stay with Luster.

"Time to git hoofing," Luster said.

When the morning star was bright in the sky they were in thick woods, on the second ridge after the slough. In the sounds of early waking they heard a dog tonguing on a trail far behind them. Luster stopped and grabbed Jed's arm.

"Listen," he whispered. "You hear what I hear?"

"I hear a hound—"

"You hear a bloodhound. I done heard it before. Every time somebody run off I heard it. They know we gone. They come to call us and know we gone. Now they set the bloodhound on us."

He started to run but tripped on the chains and fell to the ground. He kept going on his hands and knees, dragging the ball. The wire slipped from Jed's hands.

"We got to go," Luster cried. "We gonna git caught if'n we don't keep going."

Jed went after him and got hold of the wire again.

"Get up, Luster," he said. "We ain't gonna get nowheres with you on your all fours a-crawling."

Luster got to his feet and they staggered along among trees turning gray in the morning light. Jed looked at a tree with low growing limbs.

"We better climb it," he said.

"Not me. I ain't about to git treed, if'n I could git up a tree with the weight on my ankles. Peavey'd like to catch me up a tree."

They knew by the sound that the bloodhound had come to the slough and turned back, running the trail again, trying to pick up where he had lost it. Then he was silent and they knew he was going up and down the slough, hunting for the scent. It would not take him long to find where they waded out and take up their trail.

Jed looked at the spaces opening up among the trees—good

ground for running. If he had not tied himself to Luster, he could run and run. He was far enough ahead to keep on running.

The bloodhound began again, with a deep wailing baying. Luster, trying to go faster, fell and jerked the wire out of Jed's hands. Jed went past him.

"Listen to that hound." Luster was crying in a high thin voice. "I'm scaid. They gonna catch me and I'm scaid. Ain't no telling what they gonna do to me when they catch me. I seen Peavey work men over for running off."

Jed set a bee line down through an opening in the trees, running as fast as he could go.

"Jed," Luster yelled. "Come back, Jed. Don't run off and leave me, Jed. I cain't stand it to be left behind."

Jed did not answer. He kept on running, hearing the sound of his feet on the soft earth, the far off tonguing of the bloodhound, and Luster bawling. He ran till he could not hear Luster. Then he knew he had to go back. He could not run off and leave Luster alone to Peavey.

Jed broke a good club from a treetop and went back at a gallop. Luster was still lying in the dirt, whimpering.

"Get up, Luster," Jed said. "You may a thought I'd run off and leave you, but I ain't. We started together. We got to make it together. We'll keep on traveling and find us a way to cut off the chains."

Luster got up and, still sobbing, went down the opening Jed had followed before. Jed, walking close with the wire, taking the weight off his ankles, had to say something to make him stop crying.

"I been listening to him. He ain't crossed the slough. He might not be bloodhound."

"He bark like a bloodhound."

"When you're running off, any dog's bark's gonna sound like a bloodhound."

Luster took heart enough not to waste his breath on crying. On and on they went, through the woods and out to a field. The woods hid them, but they could travel faster in the field. Without a word, they cut across the field in the clear light of dawn toward a brushy turnrow far ahead.

"You hear something?" Jed asked when they were near the bushes.

Luster stopped.

"What you hear?"

"I don't hear the dog no more. You hear the dog?"

Luster's eyes were wide and white.

"He turned back."

"He give up the trail. I said he was a pot-licking hound, didn't I?"

"You said it."

With a quick look back across the field, Luster started walking again. Jed followed, holding up the ball, dragging his own feet. They could go on and on, tired and hungry, hoping some time to come to the ferry.

11

When the sun was high overhead, they were following the brushy turnrow of a field left to lie out so long that sassafras and persimmon sprouts grew in patches waist high. The sassafras buds, with tiny leaf shapes showing, were good to chew on, but they did not stop the growling hunger.

Luster stripped the buds from a sprout.

"I reckon I done et me a peck o' sassafras," he said.

Jed looked at the bushes stretching ahead of them—acres of bushes with tender, spicy buds.

"Me and you both. I et so much I ain't never gonna taste it agin."

Luster looked back over his shoulder.

"You gonna taste it all right," he said. "You don't hafta eat none to bring it back. Somebody's gonna say *sassafras* an' you gonna taste it. You gonna see me an' you walking this field with nothing to eat but sassafras. Run off—"

"Running off—"

"It don't make no difference. We dassent go back."

Luster looked down at his footing while they crossed a gully washed in the sand.

"I could eat me a belly full o' corn bread and beans—"

Jed could not let him go on.

"You ain't got no corn bread and beans. This ground ain't got no taters to grabble—"

Luster whirled and stumbled on the chains.

"I done heard enough about taters. You ain't a-gonna make fun o' me like the others. You can go on and leave me, but you cain't make fun o' me."

Jed had not meant to make fun.

"Don't be so techy, Luster. I ain't meant no harm by it. I just got to thinking about eating taters. I cain't go much longer on nothing but sassafras sprouts. I'm hungry enough to find us a house and ask for grub."

Luster looked down at the ball and chains.

"Not me," he said. "Not with these on. I ain't about to let nobody see me with these on. They'd know what I am and turn me in to the Cap'n. I reckon I'd starve first."

When they had walked again till they had to stop and rest Jed looked back over the brushy field, and ahead to another strip of woods. He stooped down and lifted the chain.

"You want me to try to break it again? We ain't never gonna get to the ferry by night this way."

Luster shook his head.

"Not till we find something to cut it with. You done tried twisting it off with that stick. You nigh about broke my legs, but the chain's still there."

He pulled up the legs of his overalls and showed his bare ankles.

"Look," he said. "Patches is a-gitting raw. I ain't gonna be able to keep going if'n it gits raw all over."

With Jed driving him, he did keep going—across fields, turnrows, strips of woods—till he dropped to the ground in a burnt-over pasture. Jed looked at the lines of woods on the horizon.

"You've got to give in," he said. "I see a break in the woods and smoke coming up. It's got to be a house there. I want to go there and get us some help. You can hide in the woods while I go up to the house. They'll give me some grub and let me have a file to cut the chains."

"They gonna ask you how come you wants a file, an' you'll have to tell 'em you got somebody hiding in the woods. Not me."

He got up and started walking, dragging the ball on the ground.

"I'm scaid," he said. "I ain't trusting myself to look at no house."

Jed followed after him but did not lift up the ball.

"You ain't got no call to be afraid I'll tell," he said. "We're both hungry. We've got to eat to keep going. You know I ain't aiming to let nobody see you."

Luster kept on going.

"You ain't no hungrier'n I be," he said. "An' you ain't got the burden I got. If'n somebody takes out after you, you c'n run like a turkey. Me, I'd git all tangled up and fall down."

When Luster would not give in, Jed had to. He took up the wire and they went on and on, leaving the smoke behind them. They waded a creek and turned aside to keep from crossing a fresh-plowed field. Jed looked for a house, but saw only a brick chimney standing where a house had burned down. It had been somebody's home place. Now it was deserted, with no sign of food left behind—only some patches of sheep sorrel sour to taste.

On the far side of the field, when they were ready to go deeper into the woods, Jed saw a kelly turning plow, set at the edge of an unplowed strip. It was dinnertime. Somebody had left it to go to dinner. He looked at the half sweep of the plow and the clevis on the beam.

"Luster." His voice was louder than he meant it to be. "Luster, we gonna get you free. You hide there in the bushes and I'll take off your chains. You got to get hid."

He looked across the field. No sign of anyone, but whoever left the plow would be back. No need to tell Luster they might be caught. Luster would go right on and they would miss the chance to get off the chains.

He dragged the plow to where Luster was kneeling in the

bushes and laid it with the sharp edge of the sweep up. He took the clevis for a hammer.

"Lay down, Luster," he said, "so's I can get at the chain."

Luster lay on his stomach in the leaves. Jed lifted his feet and laid the chains across the plow blade. Luster began to cry.

"It's hurting my ankles."

"Hold them up."

"I cain't. Cain't you see the ball's too heavy? It cuts to the quick when I holds them up."

Jed saw the chains cutting into flesh rubbed red raw, but he could not lift the weight and hammer at the same time.

"Ain't nothing to do but let it hurt," he said firmly.

At the first hammering, Luster began wailing.

"Shut up," Jed said. "Anybody can find us with you bawling like that."

"I cain't—"

"You'll wisht you had."

Knowing he had to work fast, Jed went on hammering, making first a mark and then a cut on the iron link. The chain fell from one ankle and Luster stopped crying. At last the other chain fell and Luster stood up, freed. He wiped the tears from his face with his sleeve and kicked at the chains.

"I ain't never gonna have them on agin," he said. "I'll fight like a wildcat afore they get them on me agin."

He jumped up and down and swung his legs around.

"Let's hustle," he said. "Let's git hoofing it for the ferry. We c'n make it by sundown easy, and then up the road home."

"Soon's I get shet o' the ball and chains and put the plow back."

Jed picked up the ball and chains.

"I'll be looking for the well. Ain't nobody gonna find them if'n I drop them in the well."

Slowed by the weight, he went at a fast walk back over the plowed ground. Not far from the chimney he found the well, overgrown with bushes and half-full of sticks. He dropped the ball and chains and heard the splash when they hit the water.

When he turned back, he heard a mule snort and saw a man driving a team across the field. Stooping low, out of sight, he ran along the fence row to Luster hiding in the bushes.

"We gotta go," he panted. "We gotta run."

"Ain't you gonna put the plow back?"

"We ain't got time to study none about the plow. Ain't you seen the man out there in the field? You want him to take out after us?"

Luster saw the man and, without the burden on his feet, ran through the bushes and then down a long opening in the woods. Jed kept close behind him. They came to another plowed field and went around it. Hidden again in deep woods, they stopped for breath.

"What you laughing at?" Luster asked when they were flat on the ground.

"The man with the plow. I wisht I could see his face when he finds the plow. It's a right smart gapped up from the hammering."

Luster did not laugh with him.

"I ain't finding it funny none," he said. "He'll see it and know somebody running off from the chain gang. He won't waste no time telling the Cap'n. They'll be a-tracking us agin. We better be moving."

When it was late afternoon they were again in thick woods, far away from fields and houses. Jed thought dark would catch them still in the woods, with nothing but green leaves to chew. He was ready to turn any way that would bring them to a house, but Luster kept plodding straight ahead.

They went through a fringe of pines and Jed could see the land rising ahead of them.

"Don't worry none now," Luster said. "It ain't no ways to the river. We beginning to climb the bluff now. It's a high bluff on this side so we cain't see the water yet, but we so clost now I c'n just about smell it. We git to the bluff, all we has to do is hoof it to the ferry."

12

The sun was still a hand high when they came out on the bluff and looked down on the red water running in curves and loops in the red sand. On the other side, floods had cleared away trees and underbrush, leaving a wide strip of sand. On their side, the same floods had cut the bluff from under trees, leaving them to fall and pile in drifts against the bank. Jed could smell the water. He could almost taste it on the brim of a felt hat.

"We come out at a good place," Luster said. "Look way ahead there. See the cut in the bluff? That's where wagons come down to the ferry. You can't see the ferryboat from here, so it's got to be on this side, waiting. If'n we travels fast, we c'n make it the next trip over. You ready to hustle?"

"If'n it's gonna get us some grub."

"On the other side. Ain't nothing to do but hold in till we cross to the other side."

Luster started along the bluff, following a leaf-covered trail close to the caved-off edge. Jed, a few steps behind him, kept his mind on the river and what he could see of Oklahoma on the other side. It was home to Luster, but not to him. He had to go with Luster, but he did not have to stay with him. He could see the road going up from the ferry, north. No need to tell Luster that he was going on up that road.

As he looked, a long line of blackbirds came out of the south and, rising and dipping, crossed the river, almost low enough to leave shadows on the water. Jed went faster and came up to Luster, hobbling along on sore feet.

"Look at the blackbirds," he said. "They's been a lot o' them lately. You following after them? You trying to keep up with them?"

"Purt nigh. You see way across the river where it's gray green? That's the canebrakes. They gonna roost tonight in the canebrakes. I stays a ways up the river from the canebrakes. We gonna cross over and light there and eat and sleep. You ever cross the river before?"

"I always lived by the river, downstream a ways. I crossed it agin and agin in a skiff, but never on a ferry."

He could have told Luster what it was like to cross in a skiff, and how it felt to set his feet on the wet sand of Oklahoma, but he did not.

"I wish we had us a skiff," he said. "We could cross over and not have to show ourselves to the ferry man."

Luster looked back over his shoulder.

"We ain't."

Jed looked down at the water, dark red in the red light of the sun.

"It ain't a place to swim in," he said. "Looks like too much quicksand."

"It is, and I cain't swim."

Jed swallowed hard.

"Me neither. I reckon we got to go by the ferry."

They saw first the heavy rope stretched across the river and then the wooden ferryboat pulled up in a gap cut in the sandy bluff. Then they saw the road coming down to the river.

"Ain't nobody waiting to cross over," Luster said. "I hate to think o' waiting till a wagon comes along. I'm too hungry to hold in much longer."

They passed the ferry man's cabin, set among the trees high on the bluff, and climbed down to the narrow road cut through for wagons. A man sat alone on the ferry, chewing tobacco and spitting splotches of amber into the red water. He looked dirty and old and hunkered down from so much sitting, waiting for people to come to the ferry. He shaded his eyes with his hands and watched them come down the road.

They stopped at a bar set on forked posts and Luster called to the man.

"Ferry running?"

"For them that can pay."

"We've got to cross over afore dark. We wants you to cross us over."

The man came to the ferry ramp and, holding his tobacco in a lump in one cheek, took a long, hard look at them. He'll know us next time he sees us, Jed thought.

"It's a nickel apiece to cross. You all got two nickels?"

Luster looked at Jed and back at the man.

"No, suh, we ain't. We kinda thought we could pay our way helping you pull the rope—"

The man opened his lips and let the tobacco drop. It floated at the edge of the boat, a brown ball in the red water.

"You think too fast. Look at the road. You don't see no wagons waiting to cross. I don't need no rope pulling when I ain't got no wagons to haul. You'll have to wait till a pay load comes along."

Jed, feeling the water in his mouth from hunger, stepped on the boat and went close to the man.

"We can't wait. We've got to cross over. We'd be beholden to you if'n you'd take us."

The man went to the middle of the boat and checked the hand rope and pulleys. Taking hope, Jed and Luster stood at the railing, ready to start pulling. With a quick glance at them, the man took up a boat pole and stood between them and the land.

"Where you going in sich a hurry?" he asked.

"Home," Luster said. "I live over there, just up the road a ways, close to the canebrakes. You crossed me over before, letting me pull the rope. You could be over and back easy afore dark—"

The man cut him off.

"Who be you?" he asked.

He did not wait for an answer.

"You running off from something?"

Luster stood with his mouth open.

"We—" Jed began.

"Like the chain gang?"

Jed, knowing what the man meant, started to run off the boat, to get back to the woods and hide. The man headed him off and turned him back to the river end of the boat, where Luster had run.

"You ain't going nowheres," he said.

They could see that. Before them the boiling red water, behind them a man with a boat pole.

"Somebody's been a-looking for you."

"Who?"

"You'll know soon enough."

He backed away from them till he stood on the wagon-wide ramp. The boat pole reached from one side to the other. Without turning his head, he yelled up to the cabin.

"Hey, Cap'n. Cap'n. Come on down, Cap'n. It's them all right."

Jed felt the fear run through him. He saw it in Luster's shaking shoulders. He saw the Cap'n, heavy and red-faced, come out of the cabin and half run, half slide down the bluff, with the dog on a leash behind him. He whipped out his pistol and held it on them as he ran.

"Hands up," he yelled. "Don't move from where you be."

He hit the road and, openmouthed, out of breath, ran up the ferry ramp. He motioned the ferry man to one side.

"Watch out. Don't get in the way. If they run, I'll have to shoot."

His eyes a hard blue in his brick face, he inched toward them, keeping his pistol at his hip, letting out the leash till the dog was a pace ahead of him. Luster, when he could no longer stand the fear, fell to his knees and began crying.

"Please, Cap'n," he begged. "Don't shoot. I ain't done nothing to be shot for—"

The Cap'n stood over him.

"Stop the bawling," he yelled. "I'm not about to waste a bullet on you when I'm clost enough to use a gun butt. You done something all right. You run off in the night. How come you run off?"

Luster licked at the sweat dried white on his lips.

"C'n I tell you how come, Cap'n?"

"Make it short."

"I had to. They said sixty days and costs, and it's been a heap more'n sixty days. I done waited the winter through, and I had to go home."

The Cap'n's face looked redder.

"I tell people when to go. I don't tell 'em when to come, but I sho God tell 'em when they c'n go. Did I tell you to go?"

"No, suh. I—"

"You took it on yourself, didn't you?"

"Yas, suh. I took it on myself—"

"You just up and run off, wearing your shackles. You might a knowed you'd get caught. They mostly get caught, and then they pay double. You could get the pen, running off like that. Here. Stand up."

He slipped handcuffs on Luster's wrists and locked them. Then he turned on Jed.

"You helped him run off. I trusted you loose in the tent and you helped him. Without'n you, he dassent. Without'n you to help him, he couldn't a got shet of his shackles. Answer me. You took 'em off."

"I—"

"Where'd you put them? Don't lie to me."

Jed looked at the hand holding the gun, the fingers clenched around the barrel, the butt out, ready for pistol whupping. He knew he could not lie to the Cap'n.

"Dropped them in a well."

"Where?"

"Back there a ways. You know where there's a chimbly standing in a field? It's a well clost to it. I could take you back and show you."

"I ain't a-wanting to be showed. The chains all cut up?"

"A right smart."

"Then they ain't no good to me. You got to pay for them."

"I ain't got no money."

"I ain't ast for no money. You'll work it out, doing time,

added on to what you got to pay already. You helped him. You gotta do time for helping him. Stick out your hands."

Jed held his hands behind his back.

"I ain't never—"

"Stick out your hands."

Slowly Jed put his hands out and the Cap'n locked handcuffs on his wrists. The metal, warm from the Cap'n's pocket, cut its weight against his skin.

"Come closter," the Cap'n said to Luster.

Luster came close to Jed and the Cap'n handcuffed them together. They could walk without tripping, but not run.

"That'll tame you down till we c'n get back to camp," the Cap'n said.

He marched them down the ramp and waited for the ferry man to put away his boat pole and tie up the ropes.

"I told you they'd come this way," he said to the ferry man when they were on the road. "Soon as I seen they'd lit out, I knowed they'd head for the ferry. I knowed the nigger boy'd try to go home. I let Peavey trail them with the dog down to the slough. When he come back, I says to him, 'They ain't no use wearing out men and dogs trailing them.' They come like I said, didn't they?"

The ferry man laughed a high cackling laugh.

"Don't forget, Cap'n. I holp you. I knowed 'em and I helt 'em till you come. Didn't I, Cap'n?"

"You done all that was ast of you."

With the dog close to their heels, the Cap'n marched them up the road to a clump of bushes where he had left his horse and buggy out of sight. He made them climb up and sit crowded together in the back of the buggy. He whistled and the dog, unleashed, climbed up to the seat.

The Cap'n, taking his time, untied his horse and then stood at the back of the buggy talking to the ferry man.

"It makes sense about the nigger," he said, "getting in trouble. I cain't for the life o' me see what got in the white boy. We picked him up on the road and brought him in for the night. I'd a helt him if'n I could, but I couldn't find nothing to hold him on. I needed a boy like him, so I give it a good try. Then he went off with the nigger boy. I cain't see for the life o' me why he went with the nigger boy. Ain't he knowed the trouble he's in, helping a convict run off? I got plenty now to hold him."

The Cap'n climbed up to the buggy seat. Jed could see the bulge of his shoulders and the brim of his hat. His own voice sounded strange in his ears.

"How many days you gonna hold me, Cap'n?"

"It's not for me to know. I don't set the number of days."

"How many days do you reckon?"

"I reckon it's how many months. January, maybe. December, if you're lucky, and don't be smart-alecky."

The Cap'n leaned out to the ferry man.

"It's nigh dark," he said. "We'll be moving on. It'll be late enough agin we get back to the camp, and some grub."

Jed looked across the river, at water and sand turning gray in the fading light. He should have known not to try to cross at the ferry. It was too hopeful, going by the ferry. He tried to look up the road ahead of them but could not see around the Cap'n. Without a word to Luster, he stared at the sand between the wheels and waited for the Cap'n to start the ride back to camp.

13

Jed heard the Cap'n cluck to his pony and felt the buggy start moving slowly from the bushes to the road. No use looking at the river. No use looking at Luster. He slumped down to ease the weight on his wrists, feeling the rocking of the buggy, hearing the steel tires cut the deep sand. How many miles back to camp? How many days and weeks and months ahead, doing for the Cap'n? He felt Luster's back warm against his. No need blaming Luster. They had walked into the trap together.

While he could still see the open sky over the river, Jed heard the creaking harness and grinding wheels of another rig, coming down the road at a fast trot. He felt the buggy tip as the Cap'n pulled one wheel in the ditch to let the other rig pass. He shifted his body down and put his face over his hands. He would be seen by anybody passing, but not the handcuffs—not if he could help it.

"Am I too late for the ferry?" a man asked, and Jed strained to hear his voice. "I've got to cross over so's I can find a place to put up for the night."

"I just left the ferry man," the Cap'n said. "He ain't had the time to call it quits for the night."

"I'm glad."

The way he said *glad* made Jed know it was old John, come at last to the ferry, but too late to help him. He wanted to yell to him, to beg him for help, but could not. If John saw him, he would have to see the handcuffs. The bounding would be off. John would never bound a boy he had seen in handcuffs.

He saw the horses, slowed to a fast walk, and then John, sitting under his wide gray hat with the bale of goods behind him.

He could not help turning so John would see him. He could not help yelling "John!"

"Whoa!"

John yelled and jerked hard on the reins.

"Hold it," he said to the Cap'n. "What you got there?"

"Two convicts. Running off from the chain gang. I'm the Cap'n."

The buggies stopped, back wheel by back wheel. John leaned out and looked down at them.

"I see two boys," he said. "One white, one black—"

"That's what you see, but they look the same to me. You could toss 'em up in a sack together and not be able to tell the difference."

"I'd like to try. Talking might tell."

John tied his reins to the whipstock and climbed down from the buggy. He came straight to them and, placing a hand on Jed's forehead, lifted his head to see his face.

"Jed," he said softly. "I thought it was you, Jed. How come you're in trouble, Jed?"

Before Jed could answer, the Cap'n came down from the buggy seat and stood in front of John.

"You know him?" he asked.

"I seen him—a long ways back, where I stopped a night for peddling. He looked to me like a good boy."

"He may a looked good, but he ain't—"

"What's he done?"

"Plenty. He helped the other'n run off from the chain gang. The nigger boy was a-wearing the ball and chains and they run off together. Without'n him, the other'n couldn't a run off. He cut up a pair o' shackles."

John looked Jed straight in the eyes.

"That true, Jed?" he asked.

Jed had to look down.

"I reckon."

John did not change his tone.

"I hate to hear it, Jed. I hate to see you here like this. How come you left Basil and Cannie?"

Jed tried to put more in the sound than he could in the words. "I was a-following after you—trying to find you—"

The Cap'n stopped him.

"You ain't got no call to believe him. I c'n tell you how it was. My trusty found him on the road, like he was running off from something. He acted funny, so we brought him to the tent. We give him grub and a place to sleep. I'd as lief a let him go after breakfast, but he was already gone, taking this one with him, doing something he could be sent over the road for. He holp you run off, didn't he, Luster?"

"Yas, suh, Cap'n."

The Cap'n looked at John.

"What more do you need?"

"It sounds like enough."

"They call you John?"

"Yes."

"All I c'n say, John, is don't let him take you in the way he took me."

John looked past the Cap'n, down the road to the ferry, dim in the light of first dark.

"I've got to get to the ferry man before he takes in for the night," he said. "He's got to wait and cross me over. I'd be obliged if you'd turn back with me. Cain't we all go back to the ferry and talk it over so's I'd be satisfied in my own mind? I won't hold you back any more than time for talking. You willing to do that?"

"If you ain't gonna hold me up all night. I'd as lief get these two locked up tight."

John nodded and climbed up to the buggy seat. With a quick look at Jed, he clucked his horses to a start and went on, far enough ahead of them that his gray hat seemed to be sitting on his round pack. The Cap'n turned his buggy around slowly and followed him.

John stopped at the bar across the road. The Cap'n pulled up beside him. Jed, leaning out, could see the ferry boat but not the ferry man. John climbed down from the buggy and yelled up the bluff.

"You tied up for the night?"

Jed saw through the door of the cabin the flame of a match and then the glow of a coal-oil lantern. The ferry man came to the door, holding the lantern in his hand.

"Not yet. I been holding off tying up. I come up to build me a fire in the stove."

The Cap'n climbed down and came to the back of the buggy.

"We want to come up in the light," he yelled. "We got some thrashing out to do."

"Come on up. I reckon it won't hurt nothing holding off a spell longer tying up."

Old John started slowly up the bluff. The Cap'n touched Jed on the arm.

"You all get down," he said. "Don't try no monkey business."

Jed swung his feet over the side of the buggy and slid down till he touched ground. Then he braced himself and held steady while Luster climbed down.

"Now hike yourselves up the bluff."

Handcuffed facing each other, Jed and Luster went sideways up the bluff and stopped outside the door of the cabin for the Cap'n to go in first. When he was inside, the ferry man came with the lantern and took a look at Luster. Then he turned to the Cap'n.

"Who said you could bring a nigger in my house?" he asked.

The Cap'n shrugged his shoulders.

"I ain't ast him to come in. Ain't hurting him none to stand where he is, long's I c'n keep an eye on him."

John came to the door.

"Couldn't he rest on the doorstep? We can watch him better, resting on the doorstep."

The ferry man gave in.

"On the doorstep," he said, "but not over the doorsill. He ain't setting foot over my doorsill."

Jed sat on the doorsill with his back to the facing. Luster sat on the step below him, with only his head and shoulders in the light. Jed looked away from him, at the pine planks of the walls, at the sack of flour by the stove, at the hog shank hanging from a rafter. He could smell the pine knot burning in the stove and his mouth watered. It was time to eat but John, standing with the lantern light on his face, was not thinking about eating.

"Better get down to the thrashing," he said to the Cap'n. "You got two boys here, Cap'n. How do boys like that get on the chain gang?" He looked down at Luster. "You. What'd you do?"

Jed could feel Luster trembling.

"Stoled taters."

"Tell me the truth. You did steal them?"

"Yas, suh."

"Why?"

"I got hungry."

"What was your fine?"

"Sixty days and costs." He tried to raise his hands but the handcuffs held them down. "I ain't kept count, but it's been a heap more'n sixty days."

John turned to the Cap'n.

"You kept count, Cap'n?"

"No, I ain't. I left it to Peavey."

His face got redder.

"You trying to say I done something wrong?"

"I'm not saying anything, one way or the other."

"If you got anything to say, say it to me. I'll tell you one thing. Peavey was a-fixing to turn him loose. Then he up and run off—"

John stopped him.

"Let's say he didn't run off. Let's say we could forget about him running off. How much would he owe, cash?"

The Cap'n counted on his fingers, like a trader.

"I reckon he had clost to ten days. If you wanted to, it could be squared for ten dollars."

Jed rose to his knees and went down again, pulled by Luster's weight.

"You'd let him go home for ten dollars?" John asked the Cap'n.

Again the Cap'n counted on his fingers.

"I reckon, if anybody'd show me ten dollars."

Jed looked at John's face. In the lantern light he looked older, and kinder. No harm in asking him for something for Luster.

"I wisht I had ten dollars," Jed said to John. "I ain't. I didn't even have a nickel for the ferry."

"Supposing I had it, Jed," John said. "Supposing I would pay it. Would you pay me back?"

"I'd be bounden for it."

"You know what you're saying, Jed?"

"Yes, sir."

Jed felt that he had to say more.

"I seen the chain gang. I ain't a-holding it agin the Cap'n none, but I seen the chain gang. I know what they do when the Cap'n ain't looking. I know how they'd gang up on Luster if'n you take him back. He's more'n paid for the stealing. I'd be bounden to you to get him off."

John took a wallet from his pocket.

"I believe you, Jed."

He counted out ten dollars to the Cap'n.

"Now take off the handcuffs."

Luster raised his hands to the light, pulling Jed's hands up with them. The Cap'n unlocked one and then the other. When they fell away, he stood up and slid his feet down from the doorstep. With a quick dash he could be in the bushes, hidden by the dark, out of reach of the Cap'n. John started toward the door.

"Wait, Luster," he said. "Ain't no need for you to go out by yourself in the night. We'll put across on the ferry, so you can go home."

The ferryman stopped punching at the fire in the stove.

"It'll cost you."

"How much?"

"Four bits each way. It's got to be more, crossing at night."

John barely nodded to him and then went over and helped Jed to his feet. Jed stood just inside the door with the two pairs of handcuffs, one locked on, the other hanging from his wrists. John looked at the Cap'n.

"What's the count against him?" he asked.

"Like I said before. Helping a convict escape."

"Anything before that?"

"Nothing to put on the books. I told you before. We picked him up on the road, acting like he was running off from something."

John took a long look at Jed.

"Cap'n," he said, "you say he looked like he was running from something. Jed says he was following after me. Which was it, Jed?"

"I told you. I had to come following after you. Then I seen Luster. Nobody could a gone on and left Luster."

He glanced at Luster, an outline in the darkness, a figure without face or eyes.

"I tried it once."

John came close to him.

"When?"

"It was when the dog was trailing us and Luster couldn't run. I got scared and took off by myself—"

"But you went back. How come you went back?"

"Luster kept calling me. When I got so far I could hear the dog but not Luster I had to go back."

John took off his hat and fanned his face.

"You holding that agin him, Cap'n?" he asked.

"I reckon he didn't know no better. Anyway, it ain't on the books. I wouldn't hold him, if'n somebody'd stand good for him."

"How much?"

"I calculate ten dollars more'd get me shet o' both o' them."

"How do you figure that?"

"They pay me so much a head, boarding and guarding. If'n he wasn't eating, I could let that go for five dollars. I've got to hold him for the ball and chains he lost. They belong to the county. Put five on five, you've got ten."

Again John counted out the money.

"Now take off the cuffs."

Jed shook his hands free and went close to John.

"I'm beholden to you," he said.

John put a hand on his shoulder.

"No more'n I am to you. What you did for Luster was agin the law, but I ain't blaming you for doing it. Anybody'd be glad about it but the Cap'n—"

The Cap'n stopped him.

"I have my lights. I've got to act by my own lights."

"I know. Have I been blaming you?"

"Not that I know of."

The Cap'n hung the handcuffs on his belt and went to the door. He stood looking into the night for a moment and then came back to Jed.

"For the life of me," he said, "I cain't make you out. First you run off with a nigger. Then you take up with this—"

In the pause, Jed saw something in his eyes he had never seen before.

"This son of—"

For the first time Jed heard a hardness in old John's voice.

"They mostly call me a Dutchman."

In the door, the Cap'n whispered, for Jed but not for John, "Abraham."

With another step he was outside by Luster, holding an open hand toward his face.

"You cross that river right now," he yelled, "and don't you never come back. Don't you ever let me catch you on the Texas side agin. You know what'll happen if you do?"

"Yas, suh, Cap'n."

They heard the Cap'n go down the bluff. They heard him turn his buggy around and, lashing his pony to a trot with the lines, go back up the road.

When they could no longer hear the wheels grinding in the sand, the ferry man took the lantern and went down the bluff. Luster followed close behind him. John tripped once and, to keep from falling, went down backwards, holding to Jed's arm.

The ferry man took the bar from the road and John started to climb into the buggy. Jed hung back.

"You all better go on without'n me," he said.

"How come?" John asked.

"I have to go back."

"Where?"

"To Basil and Cannie. They's things I ain't told you, and I have to go back. It's them. It ain't nothing agin you."

The ferry man had lowered the apron for the buggy and team to come on and was waiting to pull the rope.

"You don't have to go till we talk some, do you?"

"It ain't just the talking to you. It'll take a heap more time'n just talking to you about it. You minding the time?"

"No, Jed. Not for us. I was just thinking. We'd better do something else about Luster."

He went down to the boat and spoke to the ferry man.

"I cain't cross over tonight, but I said I would pay for Luster. You take him on over."

"It'll still cost you four bits each way, cash."

John went close to the lantern and counted out the money.

"It's worth it to get him home. Take him on over. I'll be here long enough to know it's done."

From the road Jed watched the ferry move slowly out on the water, with Luster pulling the hand rope. Luster had gone without a word, and Jed was glad to see him go. No use in taking up with anybody who'd seen all he wanted to see.

When they could see only the lantern on the water, John laid a hand on Jed's shoulder.

"What's the trouble between you and Basil and Cannie?" he asked.

"The watch. They found it and thought I stoled it from you. I wanted you to go back and tell them you give it to me for bounding. Nobody else could tell them I didn't steal it."

"Is that how come you followed me?"

"Yes, sir."

"They still think you took it?"

"I reckon. They ain't nobody to tell them different."

John watched the lantern, a speck of light on the river.

"We better tell them," he said. "It'll mean some backtracking, but we better go tell them. I wouldn't want them casting off about you over something that was my doing."

Hearing him, hearing his voice, strange-sounding but uncomplaining, Jed for the first time thought that it was not right to ask John to go back.

"You'll lose time," he said. "More'n a day of peddling. If'n you could tell me something to say to them."

John climbed up to the buggy seat.

"Don't worry none about the time, Jed. Time lost is time lost. Get in and get settled so's we'll be ready to go when they hit the other side."

Jed sat on the cushioned seat and leaned his shoulders against the cushioned back. He laughed, loud enough for John to hear him, and said something he had heard from Basil.

"I ain't nothing if'n I ain't a-raring to go."

14

They watched the light of the lantern slow to a stop and then start toward them again. The ferry boat had landed. Luster was on the other side, on his way home. With no call to wait for the ferry man, John turned the buggy around and, with a slap of the reins, set the horses at a slow-steady pace.

When they were away from the river, passing through a strip of pines, John reached under the buggy seat and took out a shoe box.

"Hungry, Jed?" he asked.

"I'm about past hungry, I et so much sassafras and drunk so much river water."

John handed him the shoe box.

"It's still got a little grub in it. Mostly biscuits and side meat."

"It's grub."

With the taste of the pines in his throat, Jed ate the hard dry biscuits and pieces of cold side meat. When he had finished the last of the biscuits, John brought a stone water jug from under the seat.

"Something to wet your whistle," he said.

His throat washed clear, Jed asked the question he had to ask.

"How come you done this for me, John?"

"It ain't easy, being a boy like you, so somebody's got to help—somebody that's been through it. I'm old now, but a long way back I went through it—not the same, but close enough. I didn't tell Basil, but I been the same as kicked out of all the countries I've been in but here. Not because of what I've done but what I am, with my Dutchman's brogue and all—"

"You didn't do nothing wrong?"

"Not that I know of, Jed."

"Then how come they done it? I don't see—"

"You don't have to see. Not now. You heard the Cap'n call me a son of Abraham. He didn't mean me no good by it."

Jed knew that.

"It ain't just you," he said. "I reckon the Cap'n don't mean no good to nobody. Like I said before, I had to help Luster."

"I don't blame you for helping Luster. I would a blamed you if you hadn't a helped him. The way I see it, a man's got to help them that wants to help somebody else. I reckon that's you, Jed."

Jed could not get the Cap'n out of his mind.

"Do we have to go by the chain gang?" he asked. "Ain't there some other way around?"

"I wouldn't take it if there was. We've got to pass it. If you start running agin, somebody'll turn you in and wait to ask questions till later."

"I'm afraid the Cap'n'll see me."

"Let him. It's better'n trying to pass him by. He ain't got no hold on you, no more'n nobody else—no more'n Luster or Basil or anybody else."

Jed thought of the tiehacker. They would pass the chain gang in the night, the tiehacker in the night. No need to tell John about the tiehacker.

They passed close to town, but not through town. Then they were on the road that would take them to Basil and Cannie.

"We'll make it by daylight," John said. "By daylight you can tell them you didn't steal the watch. You got something in mind to do then?"

"Go back to my bounding till October. It wouldn't be right not to go back to my bounding."

"I reckon not."

Jed had half hoped John would say something else. October seemed too far away. The waiting was more than he felt like doing. But there was nothing else John could say, not till he had worked out his bounding.

"You will come back, like you said, in October?" he asked.

John laughed.

"You can count on it. Me and you'll be on the road in October."

With his mind at ease, with the long dark road ahead of them, Jed leaned back on the seat with his head resting on the bale of goods and let himself rock with the gentle swaying of the buggy. He wanted to sleep, but John wanted to talk.

"It's always been in me to go," he said. "I told you they run me out of all the countries I went to but this'n. I didn't tell you that, run out or not, I would have gone anyway. I've always had it in me, the wandering."

15

When Jed woke he saw the house first, with smoke rising from the cookstove flue. Cannie would still be in the kitchen, at the table with Basil or washing up the dishes. Then he saw the cornfield with long rows of pale green corn—too big now for the blackbirds to pull it out by the roots. He brushed a hand across his eyes.

"You awake, Jed?" John asked. "You sure slept."

Jed looked at John, slumped against the side of the buggy, the reins held loose in his hands.

"You been driving all night?"

"All night long, but I ain't minded it none."

When they drove up to the gate Basil came to the door, followed by Cannie. She saw them and pushed her sunbonnet back to her shoulders.

"Light and hitch," Basil said. "We've et, but the old woman's still got the makings of breakfast."

He looked past John to Jed.

"Howdy, Jed."

Jed lifted the gate latch and let John go ahead of him. He saw the looks on their faces and swallowed before he spoke.

"Howdy, Basil. Howdy, Cannie."

Cannie nodded to him and went ahead of them to the fireplace room. She stirred in the ashes and brought out a few live coals.

"You'uns set here by the fireplace," she said. "I'll see what I c'n do about stirring up some breakfast. I c'n hear what you say from the kitchen."

Jed sat on a stool between John and Basil, looking at the clock, waiting for them to bring up what had to be brought up. He could hear the heavy ticking of the clock, but not the watch. Basil asked about crops and planting, and John answered him, both with a kind of dragging in their talk. When their talk had run down to a stop, Basil leaned forward and kicked at the fire with his toe. Then he looked at John.

"Where'd you find Jed?" he asked.

Jed thought of the Cap'n and the chain gang. John would have to tell Basil and Cannie about the chain gang.

"He cut me off at the ferry. I went on a-rocking down the road and he was waiting when I got there."

Nothing about the Cap'n. Nothing about Luster. Nothing about the chain gang. He looked at John and knew no more would be said about their meeting. Basil leaned close to him.

"We didn't want you to go, Jed. How come you went?"

"On account of the watch. You'uns thought I taken it. I had to get John to come back and tell you about the watch. He'll tell you he give it to me to bound me till October. C'n I see the watch, Basil?"

Basil opened the clock door and took out the watch.

"Did you, John?" he asked. "Did you give it to Jed to bound him?"

"I did, Basil, setting on the bed in the shed room."

"Well, I do allow," Cannie said from the kitchen door.

Basil sat down heavily, facing Jed.

"You're a-wanting to leave us, ain't you, Jed? John's tolled you off, and you're a-wanting to leave us."

Jed watched a dark red flush rise through the tan of Basil's face. He did not want Basil to lose his temper—not at him.

"I'm bounden to you till October, Basil. I'm aiming to keep my word."

"That's what you say out loud, but you say something else behind my back. You bound yourself to John, and he's waiting to take you."

Jed looked at John, and saw a whiteness around his mouth and eyes. He saw the nod of his head. John wanted him to go now. That was why he had come back. The road was there, and John was ready to travel it. Jed had to make up his mind.

"I ain't said I was a-going now, Basil," he said. "I've got to go sometime. I bound myself to John to go sometime. I'd admire to go right now, but I ain't."

Basil smiled and turned to John.

"He ain't got to go with you now. You don't have to have him now."

John reached his hands toward the fire.

"I ain't said he had to go now. I come back hoping you would let him go with me this time."

He stood up and turned his back to the fire.

"I reckon you ain't living in that kind of territory."

He went to the door and looked out at his rig, waiting at the road.

"He could run off from you. He left before."

Basil stared at the fire.

"He come back."

"I know. That's a sign of him—not you."

John came back and stood near Jed, close enough for Jed to hear him breathing through his open mouth.

"I've come to this way of thinking," he said. "I could pay you something to let him go now."

At his words Cannie came through the door. She gave Basil a sharp look and took a stand by the chimney place.

"Jed," Basil said, "I ain't a-going to do nothing to keep you if'n you're set on going. I need me a hand, but I made out by myself before you come. I c'n make out by myself agin a heap better'n trying to hold you agin your will."

Jed wanted to go. It was hard for him to say that he would stay. When he could not say one way or the other, Basil spoke to John.

"I wasn't aiming to ask you to buy him out," he said, "but I counted on him for a hand. I stand to lose a right smart of money if he quits me now. I reckon you c'n see that, John."

"It don't take a second look."

John was slow and careful with his words.

"How much you calculate you'll lose?"

Basil studied the question and then began to bargain.

"I cain't rightly say. It might be a good crop year, and then agin it might not—"

Cannie frowned at Basil and stopped him.

"It sure looks good now, with the corn growed to a good stand. You said so yourself, John, didn't you?"

"I said I hadn't seen better this spring."

"I'll bet on it's a good crop year," Basil said. "If'n he goes, I'd lose a lot. I reckon I cain't stand to lose that much."

John took out his wallet and held three bills out to Basil.

"Twenty-five dollars," he said. "I'm ready to pay that much for him to go with me now."

Basil looked at the money and then at Cannie. She came behind his chair and leaned close to him.

"Basil," she whispered, "I wouldn't be put on by no Dutchman."

Basil raised his hand to push the money away.

"The way I figure it is like this," he said. "Jed come up here holler'n a wooden leg and I fed him up and give him twelve dollars a month till October. I done paid him nigh about as much as you said."

He put his hand on Jed's arm.

"Ain't that right, Jed?"

Jed used Basil's words.

"Right as rain."

Jed felt Basil's fingers gripping his arm.

"You're sticking by me on that, ain't you, Jed?"

Jed saw Cannie's lips quiver and then form the word *yes*. He felt the dryness in his mouth as the word came out.

"Yes."

Basil sat back in his chair.

"You see how it is, John. Jed ain't a-going back on his word. He'll stick by me if'n I say it. He's worth a lot more'n any twenty-five dollars to me."

John put the bills back in the wallet and put the wallet in his pocket. Watching him, Jed felt like crying. He had only to say he wouldn't stick by Basil, but he couldn't, not with Cannie looking the way she did.

Cannie went back to the kitchen.

"Breakfast's ready, you'uns," she called.

Jed and John sat side by side at the table, taking the food Cannie passed to them, eating silently, with no word to say.

Basil stood in the door watching Jed fill his plate.

"It'll take you a whet to eat all that," he said. "I reckon I got time to take care o' the horses."

Basil took John's horses to the barn and came back again. Jed and John were still at the table.

"Horses needs currying," he said. "Jed, you'd better take time after breakfast to curry them down good."

Basil sat at the side of the table, across from John. He looked down at his hands, red brown against the brown of the table.

"I ain't aiming to hold nobody agin his will," he said. "I c'n see it in his face, he wants to go. You done showed you want him. Maybe we could talk some more about it."

John's eyes were on Jed and then on Basil.

"How much you asking, Basil?"

"Cash on the barrelhead?"

"Cash on the barrelhead."

Basil spread his fingers and counted on them.

"I been figuring. It cain't be no less'n forty dollars. Nobody'd expect me to give up a good boy for less'n forty dollars."

"It takes me a long time to make forty dollars—"

"You'd have Jed to help you. I ain't got nobody. With him it ain't no risk to give me forty dollars."

John turned to Jed.

"You willing to go if I'll unbound you?"

Jed thought of the money John had given the Cap'n. Twenty dollars. Now forty. Sixty dollars in all. A heap of money for anybody to bound himself for. It was John's money. John should have the say.

"If'n you wouldn't think me too beholden to you."

John laughed.

"It's a risk I'll have to take."

He took out his wallet again and counted out forty dollars. Basil took the money, counted it again, and handed it to Cannie. She counted it out loud and slipped it inside her dress.

The bargain made, John stood up.

"Reckon you could put us up for the night?" he asked. "Me and Jed'll need some sleep before we hit the road, a lot of sleep, if you don't think it's too lazy to sleep daytime and nighttime, too."

Cannie went toward the door.

"I'll fix up the shed room," she said. "John, you c'n take the cot. I'll fix a pallet on the floor."

She looked out at the buggy.

"Jed, you better bring in the goods. I got a mind to buy me a new dress."

When Jed and John were in the shed room, Basil and Cannie came to the door.

"Hand me out your things," Cannie said, "so's I can wash and iron them. I wouldn't want you a-going off not clean." She looked at John's shirt, dirty at the collar and wrinkled. "What I do for one I'm bound to do for the other."

She stepped back and Basil stood in the door, holding the watch in his hand.

"It's yourn, Jed," he said. "All wound and set. Me and Cannie wouldn't a kept it if we'd a had some way of knowing what we know now."

Jed took the watch and held it to his ear, to hear the fast ticking.

16

Long after dark, when the bale of goods had been opened and tied up again, John left them around the fireplace and went out to the shed room to sleep. Jed thought he ought to stay and talk with Basil and Cannie, but, sitting on the stool between them, seeing their faces as he had seen them night after night in the light of the fire, he could find nothing to say. He had already showed them that he did not want to stay. He could not talk of going without hurting their feelings.

When it was past bedtime for them, without saying anything he went to the gate and stood staring at the moonlit road, wondering how it would be to travel it not running from anybody or anything, not on foot, not hungry, not anything but himself.

When the moon, late rising, was bright enough to cast shadows, Cannie came and stood beside him.

"Bright as day about, ain't it?" she said.

"I reckon," he said, feeling tongue-tied.

She waited, and spoke again.

"You're leaving us come morning."

"At daylight, John said."

She touched his arm.

"Ain't you a-scared, Jed? Ain't you a-scared, going off like this, away from what you always knowed? No telling what you'll run into. You ain't never seen the kind o' harm people c'n do to you. You reckon you c'n take care o' yourself, Jed?"

"I reckon."

"We'uns'll miss you, Jed. You been a heap o' company. We'd be proud to see you, if'n you ever felt like coming back."

Her voice sounded close to crying, and he was glad when she

went back to the house, not knowing what he knew of the harm people can do.

When the lamp was out, Jed went to the barn, to the stall where John's horses slept with their heads hanging down. He rubbed his hands down their warm smooth-curried coats and dropped more corn in the trough.

Unable to give the night up for sleep, he went back to the gate and stood staring at the road. He stayed there till he felt the chill through his arms and legs. Then, knowing he had to, but not asking why he had to, he ran to the field. The young corn shoots, silver points in the moonlight, stretched away in a line too thin to cast shadows. The earth was warm and soft to his bare feet.

Again he ran, fast, light, his feet barely seeming to touch the ground—the length of the field once and then again, till his heart beat fast and the skin of his legs was alive with a tingling like needlepoint pricks. He felt good and he felt bad. Running kept him thinking about how he felt—not about staying but about going.

When the moon was beginning to whiten, he wore himself out with running and crept back to the house and to the pallet in the shed room. John was asleep on the cot, a dark lump shutting out light from the window. Jed whispered to him, to tell him that daylight was coming, but he did not answer. With nothing to do but wait, Jed lay on the pallet and covered himself with the quilt. Then he held the watch dial before his eyes and counted the hours till they would be on the road.

AFTERWORD

William A. Owens's career as a writer divides generally into three periods. From the early 1930s, when he first began to publish, until his entry into the American military during the Second World War, Owens was primarily a folklorist, and his published writings during that time record and interpret folk materials gathered from his field research.

His wartime experiences, however, what he saw of the pain and drama, the courage and cowardice that war engenders, made him realize that the writer's most important task is to understand people and their emotions and motivations, and that folklore (which, as a discipline, is uncased in the straitjacket of scholarly jargon) does not provide the necessary freedom to explore such things. Fiction, on the other hand, with its infinite variety of theme and subject matter, is a near-unrestricted medium through which to observe and comment on human conduct. Owens resolved, therefore, to become a writer of fiction.

Following the war, in pursuit of that goal, he went to Columbia University in New York to take creative writing courses. Later he joined the Columbia faculty and taught at the university for almost thirty years. The phase of Owens's writing career during which he concentrated on fiction was the 1950s and the years immediately preceding and following that decade. The fruits of his labors were certainly more than worth the effort he put into learning the craft of fiction. In a span of about fifteen years he produced three excellent novels—*Walking on Borrowed Land* (1954), *Fever in the Earth* (1958), and *Look to the River* (1963)—as well as a handful of short stories.

Over the past twenty years and more Owens has apparently

abandoned fiction in order to write a series of autobiographical volumes, including the exceptional *This Stubborn Soil* (1966) and *A Season of Weathering* (1973). But while Owens may no longer be a fiction writer, he is still a writer of narrative, and he obviously learned well the narrative techniques that he developed during the time he was expressing his vision of life through the medium of fiction.

Owens's last published work of fiction, *Look to the River*, is, I believe, one of his best books. He wrote *Look to the River*, more a novella than a novel, in a relatively brief period, a couple of months, in the early 1960s. He composed the final draft carefully and deliberately, as if, he once said, he were "chiseling the words in stone"; thus the manuscript, when completed, required only minor revisions. His painstaking choice of words in the composition of the book well explains one of Owens's great strengths as a writer: his plain but brilliantly lucid style.

Owens from the start of his career had decided that a direct, unadorned style is the best and, for his purposes, most effective means of expression. In all of his works he avoids, wherever possible, complex, multisyllabic words. He writes dialogue in the language of the people who are his characters, but does not use extreme forms of dialect; instead of mangling spelling and ordinary usage, he allows a few scattered words to suggest the flavor of idiomatic speech. In sentence structure he strives for subtle rhythms that enhance story and character. Roy Bedichek, in a review of one of Owens's books, memorably summarized the author's stylistic virtues: "The style of the book harmonizes with the tale it tells. . . . It is a lean style, for the writer husbands his words as a good tailor his cloth. . . . The author is apparently alert above everything else to economy, which is the very soul of style in everything that is formed for use or beauty by the hand of man." Though Bedichek was not referring here to *Look to the River*, his observations could well be applied to that work.

One of the most difficult things for a writer to accomplish is to appeal, at once, to many different levels of awareness. Mark Twain managed to pull off such a feat in his classic *Adventures of*

Huckleberry Finn, a book that just about everybody from sixth-graders to sophisticated literary critics can read with enjoyment and fascination. When it was published in 1963, *Look to the River* was recommended by the American Library Association as a children's book; yet few could deny that the undercurrents of meaning in the narrative, like those in *Huckleberry Finn*, challenge adult readers as well. There appears to be in *Look to the River*, incidentally, more than one oblique allusion to Twain's novel. The book takes its title, for example, from a thought that flits through Jed's mind as he works in Basil and Cannie's corn field near the Red River: "He could look to the river and think of what it was like to be on a skiff on the river" (p. 26).

In writing *Look to the River*, Owens clearly drew on recollections of his East Texas boyhood. The author himself has commented on the imaginative process from which the narrative emerged: "I had out of my own memory the chain gang scene, which I still consider the focal point of the book. I had been a boy like Jed, bound to work on a farm. I had seen peddlers, and they had stopped at our home to trade. These were the things of my region." Specific events in the novel also seem to have their roots in Owens's childhood experiences. The scene at the close of the book, for instance, in which Jed on the eve of his departure with John runs in sheer exaltation down the road and through fields shimmering in silver moonlight, is reminiscent of a chapter in *This Stubborn Soil* which describes the writer's bubbling emotions the night before a trip to the nearby town of Paris.

The fact should be understood, however, that *Look to the River* is *not* in any meaningful sense an autobiographical story. The real significance of the work, in fact, lies not in the accuracy of its reflection of the writer's memories of his boyhood, but in its allegorical implications. That *Look to the River* was intended as a kind of allegory can scarcely be doubted. None of the characters in the tale has a last name (the Cap'n has no name at all, only a title), a circumstance which indicates that, while they are individualized people, they also embody universal and symbolic values. Jed is that most familiar of allegorical figures: he is the innocent at large amid the perils of the world. Everywhere Jed turns there is someone waiting to take advantage of him, wanting to exploit his youth and inexperience: Basil and Cannie want a cheap farm hand; a tiehacker he meets after running away in search of John wants to trick him into helping move a log; the Cap'n wants to make him his "boy" servant; even Luster needs a partner to help him escape from the chain gang. Only John seems truly interested in befriending Jed because he likes his company.

John is the Wandering Jew personified. He was born in Bavaria (the rural folk with whom he does business label him a "Dutchman") where he was called Johann; but deprived of a true homeland, he had traveled all over Europe before coming to America. In France they called him Jean, in Spain Juan, in this country John. When the Cap'n, during his and John's verbal exchange at the end of the narrative, loses control of himself and almost spits out a racial epithet, the hopelessness of John's travels becomes clear; he will never, not even in an isolated, backwater area such as northeast Texas, escape the hatred that is stimulated by his ethnic origins. Nor, of course, is there any hope for Luster to shake free from the bonds of racial prejudice. Luster represents in a general way southern blacks in the early years of the twentieth century. It is symbolic that when he and Jed flee the chain gang camp, Luster still has his chains and must painfully struggle for every step forward. Like his people, Luster is shackled by the chains of prejudice, poverty, superstition, and poor education.

On a rather abstract level *Look to the River* may be interpreted as a story about cultures. John has inherited one of the world's great cultures, but because of political and social conditions he cannot claim it. Jed has a culture also, though it is considerably less polished and traditional than John's; because it is his birthright, however, Jed has assimilated his culture almost instinctively and thereby solved the problem of self-identity. Luster is the only one of the three major characters who is, by any standard, culturally dispossessed; his only culture is largely a borrowed one which, ironically enough, was hastily acquired from his oppressor.

But the lesson of the book's allegory is concrete as well as abstract, specific as well as general. The situation of the story calls for Jed and Luster to be in trouble and for John, without condescension or the hope of reward, to help them. John has managed to transcend the suffering that must have punctuated his life. Indeed through his suffering he has developed a compassion and tolerance that he could have obtained in no other way. Perhaps Jed, as a result of his friendship with Luster and of their shared hardships, will develop the same kindness and understanding. But that, if it happens, is for the future, and the reader is not allowed to know the future. All that can be said with certainty is that the tale is a parable of racial harmony, of the interdependence of all members of the human race, and of man's responsibility to be his brother's keeper. On the first and simplest level, *Look to the River* achieves its effect because it is an interesting and believeable story of a particular time and place; but its meanings, while constructed of local and regional materials, are universal.

Tom Pilkington
Tarleton State University
Stephenville, Texas

Photo by Doug Wintermute

ABOUT THE AUTHOR

One of the giants of Texas literature, William Owens demonstrates in his writing the necessity for a man to come to terms with his past and the land that shaped him. Born in 1905 in Pin Hook, Texas, a tiny community in the northeastern corner of the state, Owens grew up, he has said, "economically deprived but not culturally deprived." A life of poverty and hard work was enriched by almost daily readings of the King James Version of the Bible and by a wealth of ballads, songs and stories. Not surprisingly, folklore has been a continuing interest for Owens and formed the basis of his doctoral dissertation at the University of Iowa in 1941.

After service in World War II, Owens turned his attention to the craft of writing and began to write fiction. In addition to *Look to the River,* his novels include *Walking on Borrowed Land* and *Fever in the Earth.* His autobiographical *This Stubborn Soil,* chronicling his early years, is an important social history of East Texas, and *A Season of Weathering* continues his life as a young adult.

Owens was professor of literature and writing at Columbia University for twenty-eight years and dean of the summer session there for twelve years. Now retired, he lives with his wife in Nyack, New York but visits Texas frequently.

"I am from Pin Hook," he writes at the beginning of *This Stubborn Soil*, "and Pin Hook is a part of me. All my life has been a flight from it, but now, after many returnings, I see that it has overtaken me at last."

Look to the River captures the author's deep knowledge and intense feelings for the region of his youth.

Books by WILLIAM A. OWENS

A SEASON OF WEATHERING *1973*
THIS STUBBORN SOIL *1966*
LOOK TO THE RIVER *1963*
FEVER IN THE EARTH *1958*
WALKING ON BORROWED LAND *1954*
SLAVE MUTINY: *The Revolt of the Schooner Amistad* *1953*
TEXAS FOLK SONGS *1950*